SMOLDER
St. Martin Family Saga

Gina

Watson

ISBN-13: 978-1-941059-09-8

CONTENTS

ACKNOWLEDGMENTS

Several people made this endeavor possible. Without their support this fictional world would not exist. Thank you for all the motivation and support. Beth Hill at *A Novel Edit* is wonderfully professional and does a marvelous job with the editing process. Emily Colter and Maxamaris Hoppe at Waxcreative truly did an awesome job at conceptual design for the website that channels the St. Martin Family. Damonza.com handled cover design and formatting. Mom and Karen, thank you for always agreeing to proofread. Monica your continued support and motivation were priceless on this project. Beth B. thank you for always giving it to me straight, this is invaluable to an author. To all my students and friends, this would not have happened without your beta skills: Kayla H., Courtney W., Danielle S., Meagan W., Ruth L., Angelica L., Jenna L., Tammy S., Kelli R., Amber S. Brian, what can I say, you put up with me, for that there are no words. Thank you.

CHAPTER 1

Camp pushed against his fiancée, her stiff body preventing easy passage of his cock. Her desperate words cut through the air.

"Camp, you're hurting me."

"Kim, if you'd let me lift your damn legs, it would go in easier."

She began to cry. *Fuck*! Camp thought. It was like this every time. She was simply inhibited in the sack. He thought he'd be able to bring out her sexual desire, but it had been over a year and she was still so reserved. He felt like an ass when she cried.

"I'm sorry, Kimberly." He kissed the tears from her eyes.

She inhaled audibly and said, "You know I don't like to put my legs like that."

He knew that all too well. She didn't like anything but standard missionary. It was hard to even talk her into letting him massage her to climax, but he wanted her to feel good. He set the pad of his thumb on her clit and lightly massaged.

"Camp!"

"Hush. Let me. Your moisture will make taking me easier."

He worked her into a slow lather, but she was strung so tight. She wouldn't give herself over to him, and he hated that. He massaged deeper. He could feel the knot at her core and hear her increased wetness. If she knew, she'd probably make him stop. He could feel her holding back and the little trembles that were trying to break free. He worked her for ten minutes; she should have come by now.

"Kim, let yourself go."

Using his middle finger he traced her seam and entered her slowly. Her knees tightened, pulling her legs closer together and causing her to tighten around his finger.

"Camp, it hurts."

1

Camp let out an exasperated sigh and pushed himself to a sitting position in the bed. Kim pulled the sheet over her nakedness. Camp didn't understand her at all. She was a beautiful woman. With her assets she could be a firecracker. Instead she was a two by four, wooden and straight. He thought something might have happened to her in the past but when he'd asked her about it, she'd said she just didn't like sex. At the time he thought she'd just not had proper sex.

So he didn't rush her. They dated for six months before they'd had intercourse. To say the first time didn't go well would be an understatement. Kim cried the entire time, but he'd been more than sexually frustrated at that point. He'd been reduced to beating off in the shower and so when he finally got her where he wanted her, he pushed through her in spite of her tears—rutted into her like an animal seeking release. He'd tried to discuss it with her later, but she'd acted like nothing had happened. He didn't know what to think. He naturally thought sex with her would become easier after that, but it never happened. If anything, she became more distant with him.

***

Camp was in Lake Charles, away from home and from Kim, though he couldn't escape her in his thoughts.

He didn't know what to do for or with her. Or what to do for himself. They were engaged, but maybe . . .

No, he couldn't admit defeat again. Not yet.

He turned back to his computer, to some specs from an upcoming project, but they didn't hold his attention and right away he was again thinking of Kim.

The entire town of Whiskey Cove knew his story. He was a family man, a small-town guy. He'd been born and bred in Whiskey Cove, and he'd never left. He'd even commuted for college.

He'd met Mandy his senior year, a nursing student who'd been the lead singer in an all-girl rock band. Camp had thought that was hot. She embodied all of his sexual boyhood fantasies with her huge round breasts and lush hips, and she was an incredible fuck. It was the best sex he'd ever had. He'd married her and not six months later had walked in on her taking it doggy style in the very bed they shared.

They'd divorced. Marriage with Mandy had been the only time he hadn't thought with his head, not with the right one anyway. Mandy disappeared afterward. He'd managed to keep the reasons for their separation a secret, citing irreconcilable differences.

The townsfolk and church members had supported him, but of course they'd given their thoughts on the matter. They'd driven him to the brink with all their gossip. They'd said he needed a like-minded woman, a woman with small-town family values. Camp didn't disagree. He wanted a stable and loyal woman to build a family with. Passion would be nice but in the end, loyalty and stability were the most important qualities in a potential wife.

Kim had those qualities. She had family money and knew the importance of community and the family's role within the community, especially families like theirs, those with money, power, and impact. She'd been raised to keep up appearances. She was discreet and proper. She was socially active, and everybody knew her name. After they'd dated a few months, Camp's father and all her church elders wanted a union. Camp had wanted it too and so he'd tolerated church long enough to get hooked up with Kim. To his mind, the only reasons people attended church were to socialize and catch up on gossip.

Since he butchered it on his first try, Camp thought marriage to Kim, a woman much different from Mandy, made a lot of sense, and he always did what made sense. His brothers called him Mr. Play It Safe, but he didn't care. He thought with his head, not his heart. The last time he didn't abide by that philosophy, things blew up in his face. He wouldn't lose control again. He wouldn't put heart before head, emotions before rationalizations.

At a sound from down the hall, he looked up from his computer, but it was just one of the workmen. He was in Lake Charles through the end of the week. Right now he was supposed to be meeting a Jennifer Roberts, but she was already fifteen minutes late. Her inconsideration irritated him; she could have called.

She probably wouldn't even care that his company was paying for her to stay in a suite, just as he was. The rooms needed to be large enough to serve as temporary offices. St. Martin Commercial Construction had been hired to oversee the revamping of the casino hotel's west wing. It was to be aimed at high rollers. The developer wanted the wing to drip opulence, and this *Jennifer* had been hired to meet that design requirement. Camp wasn't impressed. He never worked well with designers, and it seemed that trend would continue.

Pleasant feminine tones hit his ears. Who was singing? He didn't mind at all, the sound was lovely and hypnotic, easing his cantankerous mood. He punched a few keys on his computer, the beautiful voice was getting closer.

Heels clacked down the hall. Not work boots this time. Camp lifted his head and that was when he first saw her, striding into his suite, humming of all things, late as she was. He took in her long wavy and windblown nut-brown hair streaked with copper highlights. Her slender neck accentuated her prominent jawline, a jawline made for nibbling. Thick dark lashes framed her chocolate eyes. Her teeth peeked through pillowy lips, and the slender bridge of her nose culminated in a button. She held her phone in one hand and clutched three portfolio folders to her chest with the other.

She wore black dress slacks and heels. Her blouse was a cream color and made of a silky material. She hadn't used all the buttons, leaving the skin of her upper chest exposed.

The woman set her folders on the table in the suite, turned to Camp, and extended her hand.

"Hi, I'm Jennifer Roberts. You can call me Jenny."

Her voice suited her. It was a bit edgy, but low and smooth, and breathiness made it sensual. He wanted to hear it again. Hell, he wanted to record it so he could listen to it forever. Camp took her small, soft hand into his.

"Campbell St. Martin."

She nodded at him. "Campbell, how about I call you Camp?"

His hand sizzled against hers. Their eyes locked, and her lips parted as she inhaled sharply. He let her hand go quickly. He would do well to remember Kim. Always think of Kim and get this chick out of your head.

"How 'bout you call me Campbell or Mr. St. Martin."

"Huh." Jenny shrugged and under her breath said, "Suit yourself, old man."

Did she just call him *old man*? "Have something to say?"

She smiled tightly at him. "Nope, I'm good. Shall I show you the room sketches I've been working on?"

"Seeing as you have already wasted fifteen minutes of my time, I should think so."

The phone in her hand beeped, and she looked down at it. She silenced it and set it on the table next to her folders.

She leaned forward and jerkily slammed opened the folders. Her blouse gaped when she moved. The top barely contained her tits. She wasn't wearing a bra, and Camp could see the shadow of one nipple. He swallowed hard. Here was a woman not inhibited by her sexuality. He felt himself growing hard. He shook off his thoughts and tuned in to her words. She was talking about balustrades and damask linens. Camp didn't care about the details, just the overall look and above all, the cost.

"How much is the cost per room?"

Her phone beeped again, and she picked it up to check the screen. Her lips thinned and her forehead creased. She straightened herself up and looked Camp square in the eye. "I don't have that information completed in detail just yet."

Camp cut her off with a raised hand. "I don't have time to meet with you until you have all of the details in order. You come highly recommended, but maybe you should tend to whatever it is that's distracting you so you can focus on what I'm paying you for."

She started to speak, but he cut her off. "You may go."

Her phone continued to beep. Camp loathed cellphones and especially people who couldn't live without being attached to one. She stepped into the hallway, ignoring his directive to go. With a worry-tinged voice, she answered her phone.

Camp sat on the couch near the windows. He couldn't believe the nerve of this woman. Did she really conduct herself like this at all her gigs? He couldn't see how she would have created such a following if she did. He listened to her say, "It's in his backpack—did you check there?"

He assumed she had a child, but he didn't see a ring. Not caring about her privacy, since she didn't seem to care, he listened to the one-sided conversation.

"Did he drink it already?" Her voice was full of concern. "Put him on the phone, please." Her voice calmer, she said, "Hey, Andrew. What's going on?" When she caught Camp's eye, she pivoted, turning her back to him. "Well, I can't do that; I'm in Lake Charles until Sunday. Remember I wrote it for you on the calendar?" She sighed. "So will you please just drink the grape?" She inhaled slow and deep. "Thank you. I love you."

She slipped the phone into her pocket and returned to stand in front of Camp. "Mr. St. Martin"—she overenunciated every vowel of his name—"have you ever had a bad day?"

She was tapping her foot, waiting for a reply. The audacity of the woman. He'd give her an answer. He stood and said, "Everyone has bad days, but one mustn't let personal life interfere with business. It's all about balance."

Her eyes grew wide, and her mouth opened on an arrested exhale. "Balance. Really?" She cocked her head. Her voice was louder and clear when she said, "Funny you should say such a thing because I heard when you found your wife in bed with another man, you botched a crucial element in the Dunbar development that ended up costing them thousands of dollars." She started to walk toward the table but whirled around and jabbed a finger toward him. "Haven't you ever heard those who live in glass houses *mustn't* throw stones? Honestly, who even talks like that?"

Camp was seething mad and jumped up, advancing on her with an anger-fueled pace. What she said was true, but he thought no one knew about the fuck-up since his father had diligently worked to cover it up. He wanted to wring her smooth ivory neck for mentioning the flaming fiasco.

"Who the hell do you think you are? You can't speak to me like that." Camp's voice was a shout.

Her voice was raspy when she said, "You can't tell me what I can and cannot do." She gathered her things and hurried to the door.

He grabbed her upper arm, jerking her back. "Hey, we're not done."

She yanked her arm out of his grasp. "Oh yes, we are. I'll send you a bill for my initial sketches and quotes."

Camp narrowed his eyes at her. Still yelling, he said, "You didn't give me any fucking quotes."

She turned and stomped up to him. "You want a fucking quote? Here's one!"

She slapped his face. Hard.

Camp couldn't believe what had just happened. He held his palm to his warm cheek. The crazy bitch had slapped him. Her eyes were large and luminous, her breathing agitated. Camp instinctively moved his hand down to his crotch to adjust his painful erection. This was far from over.

***

In her own room, Jenny packed her things. She couldn't work with *Mr. St. Martin*, so she might as well get back to her brother. He needed her.

One mustn't let personal life interfere . . . It's all about balance.

That man was the hugest dick on the planet. Her anger simmered just below the surface. She wouldn't stay here and take his condescension. She didn't need this job that badly. Besides, she was sure to be fired.

A knock at her door distracted her from her musings. "Come in."

"Room service. Your breakfast is ready."

She looked up from her packing. "I didn't order breakfast."

"Mr. St. Martin ordered it."

She gestured toward the living room. "You can set it by the couch. Thanks."

Jenny continued to pack, cursing the stuffy Mr. St. Martin. Too bad such a good-looking guy was such a horse's ass. Her phone started ringing again. She moved across the room, but she couldn't see the damned thing. She'd stormed in so angrily that she'd slung her leather-bound portfolios, along with her phone, onto the couch. She went down to her knees and peeked under the couch. Of course it was far enough under that she couldn't just pull it out.

She bent all the way down, with her chest on the ground, and stretched her hand out. When she felt cold metal, she pulled it free. She thrust her other hand against the table next to her for leverage and pushed herself up. Just as it dawned on her that the table shouldn't move so easily, the breakfast tray flipped off the table and down on top of her. She crouched on the floor covered in oatmeal, cranberry juice, and scrambled eggs.

"Just bloody perfect!" Jenny screamed.

She stood and raced to the bathroom, trying not to drip. She grabbed all the clean towels and returned to the couch. She put one towel on her head and used the rest to clean the mess. Her curses against the arrogant Mr. Campbell St. Martin increased in volume. When she couldn't soak up any more juice and had scooped all the oatmeal and eggs back into their bowls, she walked back into the bathroom, leaned on the counter, and looked in the mirror. She was a disaster from head to toe. Oats covered her long hair and her chest, and scrambled eggs decorated her shirt. Cranberry juice was sticky on her skin. She turned the shower on and let the bathroom fill with heated steam. She peeled off her clothes, threw them to the floor of the shower, and stepped into the warmth of the tiled space. She scrubbed the oats and egg from her body and shampooed and conditioned her hair twice. The hot water pelted her body, and she reveled in the sensation. When she eventually stepped out, she realized she'd used all the towels. Shit. Was there a robe?

She searched the cabinets and behind the door. No robe. She walked out of the bathroom in search of something she could use to dry off. She rounded the corner and her wet, naked body slammed into a hard, dry one. One belonging to Campbell St. Martin.

"What the fuck!" She pushed him away from her. They stood frozen. As he perused her body from head to toe and back again, his eyes smoldered and gave off a glow the color of a natural gas flame. Jenny was trying to process what had happened. Why was he in her suite?

"Turn around! Stop looking at me! What the fuck is wrong with you! You don't knock?" She was so angry, she was waving her arms and hands. Her heavy breasts swayed with her movements.

And he watched every sway.

The man stood frozen. He swallowed and with a raspy voice said, "Can I get you a towel?"

She pointed to the towels in the living room, but his eyes never shifted. His gaze was glued to her skin.

"There are no clean towels."

"How about a robe?"

Yeah, she'd kill for a robe.

He walked to the closet in the entryway, opened the door, and removed a robe. He held it open. Jenny let out an exasperated sigh and backed into the plush, white cotton.

Camp—she was not going to think of him as Mr. St. Martin, not after the way he'd checked her out—gestured to the upturned tray and accompanying mess around the couch.

"What happened here?"

Jenny raised a brow. "I was on my knees looking for something and I dumped the tray on myself."

"I see. Is that why you're walking around in your suite wet and naked?"

Jenny worried her bottom lip between her teeth. "Yeah, I had a head full of oats and a blouse full of egg."

Camp erupted into full-bodied and deep belly laughter. When he looked to her and saw she was stewing mad, it got him going again and he laughed loud and long.

When he quieted Jenny said, "I'm so glad I could amuse you."

"You don't amuse me. You frustrate and anger me."

"You frustrate and anger me too."

He sat on the couch. "Well, what on earth are we gonna do?"

"I'm gonna get the hell out of here." She retrieved her portfolios from the table.

"Is that all it takes? A few stern words and you bolt? You give up too easily."

She shot him a dirty look. "I assumed you'd be firing me, so I thought I'd save you the trouble."

"I'll say it again, you give up too easily."

Eyeing him quizzically, Jenny assumed the job was still hers if she wanted it. Looked like she'd be staying after all.

CHAPTER 2

Over the next few days Camp and Jenny remained cordial with one another and tried not to get in each other's way. Camp suspected the shit would hit the fan when Jenny found out about the cut he'd made to her fabric budget. The woman was ridiculous. The curtains need not be silk in a hotel room. Couldn't she find something that would do just as well? Satin? Linen? Hell, he didn't know. He just knew it couldn't be silk.

He stood in the foyer of the hotel where the majority of the work was currently being done and couldn't focus on the task at hand. His dreams, daydreams and night dreams, were consumed with her nakedness, still fresh in his mind as the day she'd crashed into him in her suite. Camp's brain was slowly frying. The tits that had bumped against his chest had hard points that he felt through the fabric of his shirt. Her breasts were naturally pear shaped, and her small taut nipples were dark. Her long, defined torso culminated at a mound tastefully dusted with closely trimmed curls so sparse they revealed her cleft. In seconds Camp had memorized the dips and curves of her body. Her back sloped deeply at the level of her hips that flared erotically to compensate her ass, which was spectacular. It was like a juicy apple that he wanted to sink his teeth into, and when she walked, her firm, bare ass had bounced under his gaze. Since the day he'd seen her naked, whenever she was around, he went as hard as stone.

He needed something to get his mind off of Jennifer Roberts, and so he was happy to see his oldest brother come stomping into the hotel.

"Clay." Camp extended his hand, and Clay gripped it hard and then pulled Camp in for a bear hug. Camp and Cash were the smallest of the St. Martin clan, topping out around six feet. In comparison, Clay was the male version of an Amazon. And not just tall, but muscular. As a former girlfriend had once said—and none of the brothers would ever let him live down—Clay would put the Incredible Hulk to shame.

Camp looked up into the face of his brother. "Taking a break from fighting fires?"

Clay's deep baritone ignited, "I got a couple of gigs out this way and I'm training for a certification through the next couple of weeks so you're stuck with me."

"Oh yeah, gearing up for that promotion? Am I looking at Baton Rouge's next Fire Chief?"

"Possibly." Clay nodded and turned his head left then right, taking in the surroundings. "This project is bigger than your last. I'm proud of you, little brother."

Clay tousled his hair, with Camp attempting to jerk his head from under his super-sized hand.

Camp snapped his fingers. "I'm glad you're here, I need to work up a contract for your fire protection company to inspect and outfit this place, if you have time."

"For my little brother, I'll make time." He whistled through his teeth. "You guys have been busy. I just got a contract from the site Cash is working on."

Clay placed his hand on Camp's shoulder and squeezed. "Since Dad was benched, the company would be in a bind without you. You've done well for the family."

Camp was proud that it was the St. Martin name that drove the company. He liked the work, liked that he could pick up from where his dad had taken them. "Thanks, I couldn't have kept all of the projects afloat without Cash."

Clay looked up at the exposed ceiling that was to be the entryway for the new wing. He crossed over to an exposed seam in the wall. "The old wing is outfitted with a massive fire wall." He followed the wall up to the ceiling with his eyes. "Seems to be in the ceiling too. We will have to marry the new with the old, but the materials look decent."

"Mr. St. Martin?"

Camp heard the sensual voice that never failed to excite him, heard it overly enunciate his name, as usual.

He turned toward Jenny. "I told you, you can cut the act. Call me Camp."

Her heels clicked and her breasts swayed in the silk shirt she wore and he felt his dick stir. Shit. He turned away from her to make an adjustment and caught Clay's eye.

"Oh no, sir! I wouldn't hear of it. As I was saying, Mr. St. Martin"— Camp caught Clay's smirk—"I was just informed that you cut the materials budget without consulting me first."

"I told you we might have to cut back on all your embellishments." He waved his arm dramatically across the space in front of them.

"Embellishments!" she yelled. "You've cut my budget by fifty-six percent!"

"It's nice to finally hear you speak in numbers. I've been asking you for a budget for weeks."

"I already gave you my damned budget. You scribbled on it in grease pencil and then poured your coffee over it."

Camp put his hand, palm spread, to his chest. "Accidentally spilled coffee over it. Besides, your budget was unacceptable, and you were asked for a new one. Since you never submitted what I asked for, I took the liberty of assisting you with the task."

Jenny tapped her toe repeatedly. "Mr. St. Martin, did it ever occur to you that I too have met with the developer of this project? While you may not consider the embellishments"—her voice dripped with sarcasm—"to be of much value, I assure you they have been approved by the owner of this endeavor."

"Is that so? Maybe he forgot to tell you of the quarter-million-dollar bonus I get if I keep the budget aligned and that includes wrangling in the designer." As Jenny's lips tightened, Camp stood straighter and squared his shoulders. "He calls me daily to check the bottom line. Evidently it's damned important. Pretty sure he doesn't give a fuck about your Italian sofas." He rubbed his fingers across his upper lip as he watched her face turn red. "Do you have a quarter mil, Jenny? Because if you do, I could be persuaded to let you play fast and loose with the budget and we can shut this argument down right now."

He crossed his arms and waited for her answer. She clicked over to him—God, he loved a woman in heels—and narrowed her eyes. "You're hostile and moody, and I can't work like this."

"I'm hostile?" Camp said, pointing to himself. "That's rich."

Hands on her hips, she got in his face and said, "God, what I wouldn't give to slap you across the face again."

"What's stopping you?"

They were nose to nose again, and the scent of her perfume was making him dizzy.

Thankfully, the throat clearing next to them caused them both to look up and into the questioning eyes of Clay.

"You guys wanna take this someplace a little more private so the entire crew doesn't get a free show?"

Jenny held her hand up. "Not necessary. I'll be on my way to cancel an order for twenty-one goddamned Italian sofas."

As she stormed down the hallway, Camp watched her backside sway from side to side.

***

That evening Camp and Clay went for a steak at one of their favorite restaurants.

Clay cleared his throat. "So I couldn't help but overhear your argument with . . . Jenny?" He wiped at his mouth with a white linen napkin.

"She drives me fucking crazy." Camp exhaled through clenched teeth.

Clay cocked his head. "A good woman will do that."

Camp choked on the water he'd just swallowed. "A good woman? She's combative, belligerent, insolent, hostile, aggressive, and certifiably deranged."

Clay smiled. "Now, describe your fiancée to me."

"Kimberly?"

Clay nodded.

"Well, Kim's different, you know. She's . . . Well, she's uh, she's not any of those things."

Clay cut into his steak as he said, "Bingo."

"What's your point?"

"My point, brother, is that the anger and hostility, that aggression, all of those things you mentioned, are ten thousand times better than no passion at all."

Camp thought on his words for a while. He chewed his steak vigorously and swallowed. "So you think I should marry Jenny?"

"No, I'm saying you *shouldn't* marry Kim. Even when you were a child you'd sit and stew. You'd keep yourself reserved and controlled. Jenny makes you buckle, and I've never seen you so flustered. Your interaction with her struck me as such a stark contrast to how you are when you're with Kim." Clay shrugged. "Jenny seems to be under your skin."

Camp rested his forehead in his hand. "First Cash and Isa, now you. Nobody likes Kim."

"I like Kim just fine, but you guys aren't meant to be. You shouldn't rush into marriage, at least. Maybe consider extending the engagement. It will be your second marriage."

"Why does everyone keep telling me that as if I don't know?" Camp was frustrated, but didn't know how to relieve it. "Plus Jenny's troublesome and defiant, not unlike a loose canon. She'd just be an aggravation."

Clay nodded. "Maybe. Or maybe she would make you crumple to your knees."

Camp's mouth fell open, and he shook his head. "Never happen." But what if it did? He asked Clay, "And that's a good thing?"

Clay shrugged one shoulder. "It can be. I, for one, love passion like that in a woman. And notice that she is only like that with you, and you with her. It's a chemical thing. And there are ways, as you well know, to stoke such flames."

Camp's eyes went wide. Clay had lost his mind; the smoke had finally gotten to him.

***

When Camp returned to Whiskey Cove, he drove straight to Kim's place. He needed to see if there was any passion to speak of. Like Clay had said, the evidence of any desire at all would be better than none.

He rang the bell at her front door. She answered in her white plush robe, fresh from a bath.

"Come in. Can I get you some sweet tea?" Her sweet tea made him gag; it was so sweet, his jaw locked as soon as the first drop hit his tongue.

"I'm good, thanks."

Kim turned off the television. Then she rounded the coffee table, picked up a bottle of nail polish, and screwed the lid tight. He noticed her freshly painted nails as he took the chair next to the fireplace while she sat herself on the couch.

"Come over here." Camp patted his knee, indicating where he wanted her. Her color deepened as she joined him. That seemed a good sign.

She stood before him, fiddling with her robe. "What is it?"

"I want you in my lap."

She looked around—anywhere but at him—and grasped the collar of the robe, securing it higher around her throat. "My toenails are wet."

He was getting more irritated by the second. What did she think he was going to do to her? Recalling how carefree Jenny was with her nakedness, he reached up and pulled the sash on her robe and slid it from her body while she gasped and reached to cover her breasts and pussy.

"Let me look at you."

Her eyes were large and unblinking.

Camp's voice was a whisper when he said, "You can do it. Move your hands."

She closed her eyes, but kept herself covered. Camp didn't understand her—was it him?

"If you won't even let me see you naked, I don't understand how we're going to be married."

At his words she lowered her hands and stood before him. She kept her head down, and he was unable to read her eyes, but she was beautiful, there was no denying that. He looked from her large plump and firm breasts to the sensual curve of her hips and the juncture at her thighs. Her nipples were not erect, and he wondered what that meant since he'd always thought of those as a barometer of a woman's arousal. Was she not aroused?

"Do you want me?" His voice was low and raspy.

She sniffled as tears fell from her eyes. "I love you; of course I want you."

Her tears made his chest burn. He felt like an ass, so he gave her the robe. She quickly put it on. He didn't expect anything from her if that's what she worried about. He would gladly just eat her out. Anything to have her completely let go and let the passion overtake her.

He held her hand in his. "Let me go down on you, I want to taste you."

"You know I'm not comfortable with that."

He knew all too well as it was one of his favorite sex acts and she'd yet to let him taste her. Camp sat and watched the woman he was to marry as his fingers rubbed across his brow.

"What forms of sex are you comfortable with?"

She shrugged and turned as red as a cherry. "I don't mind you on top."

"You don't mind?"

She shook her head.

"But that position isn't comfortable for you."

With her eyes closed tight, she said, "I bought something."

Her admission had Camp intrigued. He followed her into her bedroom and watched her pull a tube of lube from her bedside table drawer. "Here." She placed it in his hand.

She climbed into the bed with her robe on, and he climbed up after her. He parted the robe and drew her nipple into his mouth. He was curious to see if it would harden at his touch, and so he grazed the tip with his teeth and felt it pucker. Okay, that response was normal. He kneaded her other breast with his free hand. He would have appreciated a moan or something, but she never did that. Instead she whispered, "Apply the lube."

Either she was getting aroused or she wanted to get it over with. Either way, Camp needed to find something to hold on to, something that said marriage with Kim made sense. He squirted some of the lube into his hand and massaged her with it. Then he rubbed his glistening hand over his cock until it was slick. Still, she was small and he was large and if he could just position her better, sex wouldn't be painful, but she always refused. He used his knees to settle between her legs. He'd try one more time. He slid his hands under her ass and tilted her up, spreading her legs wide, and to his surprise she didn't protest. He would have liked to start by massaging her to climax, but he didn't want to press his luck, so he slowly entered her tight, slick passage.

She didn't make a sound, but he gasped from the struggle to hold back. After sheathing himself all the way inside, he gave her a minute to accept his size. When he could hold back no longer, he pulled out and thrust in again. He drove in and out of her repeatedly. His pace became more aggressive and erratic, and he reached down to massage her clit, feeling her tightly controlled body tremble. He felt the increased wetness and knew she'd climaxed, though she showed little reaction. He'd never had so much trouble getting a woman off. When Camp came inside her, he looked to her face. She had her eyes closed tight as tears leaked from under the lashes. The situation seemed hopeless.

As Camp drove to his house twenty minutes later, he was conflicted about his relationship with Kim. He suspected he'd rushed into an engagement to satisfy his need to be with someone—he hated returning to an empty house. He'd always imagined coming home to dinner bubbling on the stove, kids running around screaming, and a loving, passionate wife. Kim would give him that—except for the passion. And what about love? Did she love him? Did he love her?

No, he didn't think that he did. He felt sympathy for this woman who was unable to let go and trust him with her body. If she couldn't do that, would she trust him with other things? Her life, her future?

As he pulled into the driveway, he saw Cash's truck and Isa's Camaro. That meant she was staying over again. Isa was his friend and Cash his twin brother, so of course he couldn't be happier for them, but their intimacy in all things—even the most mundane tasks—and their consideration for one another made his situation more pronounced.

He'd asked Kim if she wanted to see someone about her issues. She didn't understand his suggestion. He'd told her she recoiled at all things sexual. She'd told him she just didn't like sex. Camp had asked her about other men. There had been two. He knew one of them—Jerry Joe. Had she thought they were a romantically involved couple? He didn't have the heart to tell her that Jerry Joe was gay. When he asked her about the second guy, she'd told him he left to pursue his calling at seminary. Missionary position indeed.

What was it Cash had told him? Death was preferable to a lifelong marriage with no passion. Camp sighed loudly in frustration as he headed toward the front door. He thought about Jenny and how just her presence caused him to become hard as steel—she was gasoline and he was fire. To stay hard tonight he'd actually been thinking of her naked body, the heavy, swaying breasts and erect nipples. He'd climaxed inside Kim, but only because he'd been reliving Jenny's hand slapping him across the cheek. What a fucking mess. He was engaged to one woman and yet coming at the thought of another. Shit.

He knew what he had to do and once that task was completed, he knew what he had to have.

He wasn't a fool, and wasting time was foolish. Not going after what he needed was foolish too.

Yeah, he was all about going after what he needed.

***

Camp didn't want the situation with Kim looming over him, so he'd called her at lunchtime the following day. He was on his way to her home now to break off the engagement. He couldn't live like a monk with her. He was no missionary and he definitely wasn't gay.

15

As they sat on the couch in Kim's home, she handed him the engagement ring he'd given her. He hadn't had to say anything; she was breaking it off with him.

"Camp, I can't satisfy you. You know how I was raised. I feel dirty doing those things."

Her parents were strict, but Camp thought that she, like most people raised by parents that were too unyielding, was ready for a rebellious stage. Once again he'd been wrong about a woman.

Her head hung low. "You've been so patient with me and you're very kind. The truth is, I don't want to be laid bare and I don't want you to make my body hum, as you say."

God, she couldn't even look him in the eye.

"I like all the layers of clothing. I don't want my body to be exposed. It makes me uncomfortable."

That was the understatement of the century. Camp also thought it was a waste since she'd been given a body that could rival any supermodel's.

"My parents had pushed me to accept your engagement. I thought I could learn to be all the things that you wanted, but your . . . your raw sexuality scares me. You deserve to be with someone who can satisfy your desire. I love you as a sister loves a brother. Let's not be sad about this. It wasn't meant to happen for us."

Utterly relieved, Camp sat forward and took her hands in his. "Kim, I wish you all the happiness in the world, and I will always be here for you, just as a brother should be." He could do that, and he sensed that she really did see him that way, as a brother or a friend. "If you ever need anything, you can come to me any time."

On the drive home Camp experienced a calm and satisfied contentment he hadn't felt in over a year. He wondered at the push by society and parents for children to do something that was clearly not in their best interests. He knew Kim had felt that push, just as he knew she was now enjoying the same relief he felt. He was convinced that she would be okay. But Kim was the past, and he didn't intend to spend any more time thinking of her.

An undercurrent of excitement thrummed through his body. He couldn't wait to get to Lake Charles and to Jenny.

CHAPTER 3

Camp, ticked off, was headed to Lake Charles. He needed to get to the bottom of some delivery mix-up, and he hated walking in to issues cold. He always had his deliveries running like clockwork; it was all about diligent scheduling. He would get to the bottom of this screw-up and determine who was responsible.

Renovations were in full swing when Camp arrived at the site. Dumping his bag in his suite, he could make out Jenny's voice. God, that warm and rich voice as comforting to him as coffee with cream, he'd never tire of listening to it. They'd been leaving the connecting double doors open between the suites. Occasionally, she would sing, particularly, he noted, when she was closely focused on something. He delighted in the deep creamy and throaty rasp that carried her velvety voice through the airwaves.

Currently she was in the next room explaining to the tiler the star-shaped grid pattern she wanted for the bathrooms.

John, the project manager, walked into Camp's suite just moments after he'd arrived.

"Camp, take a look at this."

"What is it?"

John handed him a form. The earth-moving equipment that would be needed for the outdoor pool and garden area was here now. The only problem was, the crew wasn't due until next week and an extra week's rental on at least forty heavy trucks and machines totaled in the hundreds of thousands.

"It's a week early. Who authorized this delivery?"

John slapped another piece of paper on top of the one in his hands. "Not sure; it's illegible."

The signature was illegible, but Camp had come to recognize it. Jenny had accepted delivery of the equipment. What the hell was she doing making decisions like that without contacting him first and why the fuck was she involved at all with equipment orders? His blood boiled. He bellowed, "Jenny, get your ass in here now!"

Jenny walked through the attached doors. "I don't appreciate being summoned by an expletive, if you don't mind."

"Do you want to explain this?" He held the invoice in front of her face.

Jenny took the paperwork from his hands. "Oh, you weren't here and they needed to deliver their equipment, but they wouldn't without a signature, so I signed for you."

Camp inhaled deeply, willing himself not to yell. The quick pep talk didn't work.

"Do you know what your mistake is going to cost me?" Jenny's lips tightened and her hands balled into fists. "I'll just take it out of your budget, what do you say? Should be about two hundred thousand. You can say goodbye to your stupid entry fountain and ridiculously oversized lobby fireplace that won't ever even be lit in southeast fucking Louisiana!" His nose was centimeters from hers.

Face red, she pressed even closer. She pushed at him with what seemed to be all her might and managed to move him only a couple of inches. Then she stabbed a finger into his chest, and her eyes narrowed to tiny slits as she placed her free hand on her hip. "You're the one who dropped the fucking ball. Had you been here tending to your shit, I wouldn't have had to take care of it for you."

Clay must have heard the commotion because he'd entered the room. Stepping close, but not quite between them, he said, "Guys?"

In unison they replied, "Stay out of it, Clay."

Clay threw his hands in the air and backed out slowly, leaving them to have at one another. Camp caught the smirk on his face, but he simply channeled that ire into his anger at Jenny. Everyone else vacated the area, slamming both his outer door and hers. The echoes sounded loud in the suddenly quiet suites.

"You should've called before you signed. Better yet, you should stick to what it is you think you know. Decorating."

Jenny's shoulders squared off, and she yelled, "The word is *designing*."

"Whatever. I'm taking this money out of your budget." He moved to the table where all his paperwork was organized to perfection. He pulled the budget for *decorations*. "Let's see what we have here." He picked up a pen and scanned the budget. "Ah yes, here it is—one ridiculous big-ass fireplace." He drew a thick line across it with the pen. "Done!"

"You're a fucking lunatic!" Jenny screamed. "You're so inconsistent. Just last week you were hollering at me for *not* accepting delivery of sheet piling."

Camp bent over to put himself on her level. He shouted, "That's

18

because I fucking told you to sign for the sheet piling."

Jenny violently shook her head. "No, you said to sign for the pool and garden deliveries. What the hell does sheet piling have to do with pool and garden? Earth-moving equipment I know is necessary, so I signed this time and you still aren't happy. You're fire and ice, hot one minute and cold the next. I never know where I stand with you."

Camp howled and raised his arms, surrendering. "You're fucking useless!"

Jenny's thick lips thinned and her eyes narrowed to laser fine points he was sure she was using to induce an aneurism in his brain. She abruptly lunged forward and cleared the contents of his makeshift desk in one quick swipe. His organized papers landed in a jumbled heap on the floor.

His blood boiled up and over. He actually felt it push beyond his limits. Fire and ice? Fuck ice, he was all fire, and he'd incinerate them both if she couldn't put it out in time. In a standoff, they faced each other from opposite sides of the table. Together they dove for each other, meeting in the middle and crashing onto the worktop in a tangle of roaming lips, fingers, hands, tongues, and teeth. Camp yelled, "Fuck!" His hands were under her shirt. She pulled at his until she had it off and threw it down to join the papers on the floor. He squeezed at her breast hard, and she bit down fiercely into the soft tissue of his bottom lip. He ripped her shirt open with one hand and buttons went flying. He had her by the hair, and he closed a bunch in his fist until she cried out. He pulled her off of the table with him until they were on the floor. Jenny took his nipple between her teeth and bit hard.

"Dammit!"

They rolled and then both jumped up, gaping at each other as their chests rose and fell from their exertions. She took her time taking in his naked chest. His pants had slipped low during their rumble and now they rested at his pelvic bone. Her eyes were fixed on his pubic area as she panted, her mouth open slightly. He had an unobstructed view of her breasts and saw when her breathing hitched and became short, labored rasps. Her tongue darted out and traced her lips as her gaze narrowed in on his erect cock, and she'd yet to blink or move, just unabashedly stared, like an animal, like a feral seductress who wanted to devour him.

She stood there with her ripped shirt hanging from her body, making no move to cover herself. Her nipples were so hard they could cut metal. And then she moaned. The sound was low and soft, but he heard it, and his cock jumped in her direction.

She ran to him and jumped into his arms, fastening her legs around his waist. She groaned as she took his mouth. She plunged her tongue in deep and he sucked it, tasting her. They were a tangle of teeth, tongues, and lips as they consumed one another. She reached between them and grasped his erection. She first tightened her fingers and then she slid her loose fist down his length. His cock jumped. God, she was measuring him. She was actually checking out his length and thickness. Their kiss broke apart when she gasped as she appreciated his size. Her eyes grew wide. Camp smiled at her provocatively, and she responded with a sultry smile of her own.

She cleared her throat and slid down Camp's body. She pulled away and clasped her shirt together, closing her eyes, taking a deep breath and exhaling on a sigh. When her eyes opened, they were slow burning embers. She turned and started to walk away. Not a chance in hell! He gripped her hips from behind and snaked his hand up her torso, pushing her back against his naked chest, and fondled her breasts. Never loosening his hold, he walked her to the table and forced her down on it. Reaching his hands around her waist, he unbuttoned her pants and slid them down her legs. When they fell to her ankles, Jenny kicked them off. Her shoes had been lost somewhere in their battle.

Camp's cock tightened at the sight of her ass in a black lace thong. She had the sexiest ass he'd ever seen. It was firm, ripe, and juicy. He hooked his thumbs into the thong and slid it off. He watched her lower her chest to the table, effectively lifting her ass and exposing the lips of her sex to his gaze. She arched her back even more when she got into position, and all he could do was watch her suggestive movements. He was frozen in place; she had him entranced. She turned her head over her shoulder and made eye contact with him, and then she moved one leg to emphasize her offering. He knew he would look back on this moment his entire life as the single most erotic thing that had ever happened to him. He let out a snarl and planted his hands on her luscious ass cheeks and spread her open so he could see all of her. She pushed back while he had her spread and rubbed herself on his still-clothed dick.

She whispered, "Do you like what you see?"

He would have to be deranged not to. "Yeah," was all he could manage between rapid breaths.

"Do you want me?"

Again, deranged not to. "Yeah."

"Well, take your pants off and fuck me."

A tortured sound was ripped from his throat. He was out of his pants in an instant. He wanted to taste her so bad, his mouth was filling with saliva. So he spread her again and licked the length of her seam. Using his thumbs he opened her even more, exposing her pink center. He licked her glistening core and pushed his tongue into her warmth. He felt her fingers come up to massage her clit. He licked her fingers too.

"Mmm."

She moaned, raspy and deep, as he pushed into her deeper with his tongue. He pulled back and slid his wide tongue over all of her and pulsed there while she massaged her clit.

"God, Camp. Mmm . . . I want to come on your tongue."

She was moaning and talking dirty, and he loved her for that. She was completely uninhibited. He'd never met a woman like her.

After he lapped up every drop of her cream and he couldn't take it any longer, he fisted his erection at the base and lined it up with her entrance, of which he had a front row view. He pushed in slowly, and she gasped and whimpered. He released the remainder of his length from his fist and pushed into her all the way to the root.

"God, yes." She rocked him gently.

Using her hips, he pushed her forward and pulled her back onto his cock while he simultaneously thrust. Once she was fully seated, he released her, grasped her shoulders and found a hard rhythm that he sensed she wanted and knew he did. Using the grip he had on her, he pulled her down and pumped into her vigorously—so vigorously the table was bumping against the wall to their rhythm.

She reached through her thighs and massaged his balls while she breathlessly whispered, "I'm going to come."

His stomach was in knots hearing her talk like that. Her words took his breath away, and he knew he hadn't been doing a good job of responding in kind.

"Give it to me, baby," he said low and raspy as he pumped at a steady pace.

She released a guttural sound, and her body shuddered beneath him. Her contractions tightened the inner walls that gripped his penis, and he exploded into her. He came with vigor and when he pulled out, ropes of his come dripped down her thighs. He grunted at the sight that had him instantly hardening again. He placed his hand to her lower back and said, "Wait here."

He padded into the bathroom, turned on the faucet, and lifted a towel from the rack, then moistened it while staring at himself in the mirror. He had a sliced lip, dried blood on one nipple, and scratches on his shoulders and neck. "Damn." They had gone at each other like they were at war. Part of it could be attributed to their frustrations with one another regarding the building of the casino, but he sensed there was another catalyst surrounding her behavior. He wanted to know everything about her and thought maybe she'd share room service with him and sleep in his bed so he could hold her while she confided in him. He also thought she should know why he'd been frustrated with his life before he met her. He'd recently dealt with his problems head on—had she confronted hers? He knew he was making assumptions but he sensed she was dealing with a few issues of her own, given her aggressiveness.

He returned to her waiting body. He put the cool cloth beneath her thighs and wiped gingerly. She gasped at his touch. When he had her cleaned, he pulled her up from the table using her upper arms. He turned her to face him. Her ivory skin showed his handprints where he'd grasped at her breasts.

"Uh, we went at it rough. Are you okay?" He raised a brow at her.

She let out a hollow laugh. "Please, Camp, don't get all sentimental now. I can take a little rough fucking every now and then."

Dumbfounded, he frowned. That wasn't the reaction he'd been expecting. He'd thought their connection was a game changer. "So you've done this before then?"

Her brow furrowed as she studied him. "Sex? Well, yeah, I am twenty-seven years old."

"That's not what I meant. Do you have sex with all the site contractors you work with?"

Her eyes followed the lines of his body as she slowly took in all the parts of him. Her nipples hardened before his gaze, but then she shook her head and focused on his eyes. "No, I've never fucked any contractors. Not until you."

Camp slammed his palms into the table. "I didn't say *fucked*."

She snorted derisively. "No, but it's what you meant."

"No, it fucking isn't!"

"I've got to go." She was collecting her clothing from the floor when he took her wrists into his hands and pulled her to him.

"Why are you fine with ignoring what's going on between us? Is it your son, Andrew? Are you with his father?"

"What? No." She shook her head.

"Stay with me."

She inhaled sharply, "Camp, what more could you possibly want from me? I've given you everything I have to give. I'm tired and hungry. I need to get something to eat and call it an early night."

"Eat here. Sleep here."

"You can't be serious."

Camp moved in front of her, blocking the path between their rooms. "I'm deadly serious."

"Well, I don't need you to do this, okay?"

"You may not need it, but I want it."

She offered a tight smile that didn't reach her eyes. "You want what, exactly?"

Exasperated, he pushed away from her. "Fuck, Jenny, I just wanted you to stay the night with me. That's all."

"That's exactly my point." She stalked off with her clothes balled into her hands. When she crossed the threshold to her room, she slammed the door and turned the bolt to lock it. Camp grabbed the nearest object, which happened to be a lamp, and threw it with all his might at the closed door.

Camp's cellphone buzzed, so he picked it up from the floor and saw several texts from Clay.

Can you keep it down? Whatever ur taking her against is bumping the wall that we share and I'm trying to study for my certificate. The last one, Camp knew, was sincere. *You ok, bro? I heard something break, so let me know.* Clay was only a few years older than Camp and Cash, but he took his role as the eldest seriously. He was very protective of the St. Martin clan.

Yeah, man, just gettin mind-fucked.

Clay replied, *Ouch, that stings. I'm here if u wanna talk.*

No, he didn't want to talk. And what he wanted to do needed a woman, not his brother.

He hurled another object against the door. This time a pillow.

Unsatisfied, he stomped off to the bathroom and slammed the door.

He'd never been one to throw things and act irrationally. That woman made him crazy.

***

Jenny jumped when she heard something crash against the door. A lone tear escaped her eye. She'd love nothing more than to share dinner with Camp and sleep the night away in his arms, but she couldn't afford to do that. She had her brother to think about. He needed her, and she'd learned that a man didn't fit into their lives. She didn't want to disappoint her brother or Camp and decided it would be too risky to let down her guard. She had needed Camp tonight and would need him again, and she hoped that they could be intimate and leave it at that.

She played back his kiss and recalled how it was like fire and ice, fast and slow, hard and soft, shallow and deep. She'd been lost in the magnitude with which he tended to her needs. There was no doubt he could be a real fucking bastard, but she'd never been with a man with so much rugged virility. Thinking of his sexy smolder had the knot at her core tingling with need.

God, his trim, taut, and smooth body took her breath away. When he stood shirtless with his slim-fitted trousers down around his hips and that smoldering angry stare in his eyes, her mouth had gone dry because all of her moisture pooled between her legs. His body was slender and his muscles were so tight, it gave him a quality that she associated with masculinity. He even had veins across his lower abdomen. Those veins she'd followed with her eyes as they'd culminated somewhere in his pants.

Too bad he'd taken her from behind, not that she'd minded at the time. But she hadn't been able to watch his body as he'd pumped into her. She'd felt him just fine, but he was gorgeous and the visual would have been a plus.

She would need more, so much more. She thought about the huge error she'd made that cost him thousands of dollars. She hated that she'd messed up, but mostly she hated that he thought her to be useless. She vowed to come up with some sort of solution but for now she'd order some room service, have a nice long hot bath, and then she'd crawl in bed while it was still daylight out. She hoped she'd dream of Campbell St. Martin.

CHAPTER 4

It was the third day since they'd had sex, and Camp had yet to see Jenny. It was morning and Clay joined Camp in the suite for breakfast. They sat at the table, reading newspapers. When Clay's food was gone, he asked, "Will you be eating that"—he gestured to Camp's untouched plate—"or those damn Oreos?" Camp held up the six-count package of Oreos and shook it. Clay nodded and plucked the glass of milk from the tray, setting it in front of Camp. Camp dunked an Oreo into the milk.

"Do you wanna talk about it? You've been brooding for three days."

Camp looked at his brother. The fork in his fingers, in proportion to his fist, made him look like a giant. He guessed it would take more than two trays to fill up that massive body. "I want her."

"You never could do casual sex. What's your plan? I know you have one brewing."

Camp was a planner. He'd already made it to plan C where Jenny was concerned. "She says she doesn't need me, but she's wrong. You should have seen how much she needed me the other day. And where the hell has she been?"

"Actually, I may have some insight into her whereabouts." Clay took a long swallow of coffee. "She's been overseeing the removal of the equipment delivery."

Camp, leaned forward, frowning. "She what?"

"She called the company and explained what happened with the delivery. They told her unless she could figure out a way to get the equipment over to the next customer in line, the YMCA, that she'd be stuck with the additional rental charges." Clay ate a strip of bacon in two bites, then picked up another and waved it at Camp. "Turns out, the YMCA is a mile down the road. However, if you access it through the back of the casino's lot, you diminish the distance to two hundred yards. She had the workers drive the equipment over and she drove them back until every last piece was moved. She got the cost down from two hundred thousand to under ten. Still an error, but much less of one now."

Camp was dumbfounded. He scratched at his head. Why had she not told him? "When was this?"

Clay cocked his head. "Two days ago."

"Why wouldn't she tell me? Why wouldn't you?"

Clay shrugged. "It's her business to tell. I don't know why she didn't tell you other than we've seen it's in her nature to be defiant."

Camp's hand tightened around the bag of Oreos, and it was only when he heard them crunch that he realized he was tense. "God, I want her. I need her like I need food for nourishment, but she won't speak to me."

Clay shrugged. "You could always bring her to the club. Fuck some sense into her."

"I'm not sure she would consent to that."

"I don't know, she sounded pretty feisty the other day. You already know she likes to fight."

Camp was the only brother who knew about Clay's controversial sexual cravings. He was a member of a local sex club in Baton Rouge. Clay liked to dominate women. Camp just didn't know to what extent. Camp thought about tying Jenny down so that she was at his mercy. He'd sensed she was withholding information and now that he'd had sex with her, he thought it would be fairly easy to elicit information from her by withholding her orgasm.

He drummed his fingers on the table. The more he thought about it, the more he imagined she wouldn't fare well at all in that kind of situation.

He found himself nodding, imaging her begging him to make her come.

"So you're considering it, then?"

"What?"

"I said you're considering dominating her. I could tell by the way your eyes dilated. That and the slow grin that just took over your face."

Camp nodded. "Yes, I'm definitely considering it. In fact, I'm beyond considering. I'm fucking doing it." He met Clay's steady gaze. "I may need some pointers."

Clay smiled and pushed back against his chair. "Welcome to the dark side."

CHAPTER 5

By the end of the week, Camp was back in Baton Rouge and feeling defeated. He'd asked Jenny out three times and been completely shut out. She offered no excuses, simply said she couldn't get involved. He'd asked questions and she'd said no to all—*Was she seeing someone? Was she not attracted to him? Was she worried he wouldn't care for her son?* Yet he'd caught her watching him more than once, and she'd either been licking her lips or her eyes were hooded. What had she been thinking?

Hell, he knew what she was thinking—the same thing he'd been thinking. So why turn him down?

She'd kept to herself, but he'd told her how impressed he'd been with her turnaround on the delivery error. He'd attempted to apologize for calling her useless, but she'd shushed him with her hand in front of his mouth. She'd said she had screwed up and that calling her useless rather than firing her on the spot showed great restraint on his part. The next day he'd found a ceramic Oreo cookie jar on his desk. Inside were individually foil-wrapped Oreo cookies. She'd included a card that said she appreciated his restraint and also his attention to her needs, but the site crew had all left for the long weekend before he could get to her.

He didn't understand Jenny, but he now had new information on her. Clay had found out that she sang at a jazz lounge in the New Orleans French Quarter. The drive to New Orleans from Baton Rouge was about an hour and twenty minutes. Camp was leaving at seven thirty to head her way.

As Camp drove, his thoughts were consumed by Jenny's smell, taste, sound, and touch. Thinking of her low sultry voice, he could understand why she sang, but what he couldn't figure out was why she wasn't dedicated to one job or the other. He'd come up with a handful of reasons for why Jenny might moonlight as a lounge singer and work during the day as a designer, but he knew nothing for sure. He didn't know how much money she made at her day job—he knew what he was paying her firm, but he doubted she received even half of it. Maybe she wanted to break out and become a famous singer. But if so, wouldn't she need to be in Los Angeles or Nashville? One of the more upsetting reasons he thought up was that she liked the attention singing garnered her. Male attention, that is. He wouldn't have thought such a thing if not for his first wife, Mandy. She used her position as lead singer in a female band as a platform to lure men to her bed.

It was nearly nine when Camp arrived at the lounge, and an older man with a saxophone was just wrapping up. Camp took a table in the middle of the floor. A waitress came, tried her hand at flirting, but he shut her down quickly and ordered a single malt scotch with spring water. When the waitress finally moved, his breath hitched in his throat. Jenny was taking the stage in a stunning cream-colored dress. She'd transformed herself into a golden-era goddess in a gown that flowed like water down to the floor. The material clung to her curves, and the plunging neckline showed off her flawless skin.

He doubted she could focus on any of the audience given the strong spotlight that shone on her.

She gracefully took her seat at the piano and spoke into the microphone.

"Good evening." Her low sensuous voice reverberated through the room. "How is everybody on this warm and humid Friday night?" Catcalls and screams answered her. "All right, then the stage is set. Order a drink, sit back, relax, and enjoy the music."

He recognized the song within the first two chords—"Cry Me a River." Her voice was smoky and rich and flowed like melted chocolate. She had her audience entranced with her sensual nuances. No one talked, all eyes were on her, and in that moment Camp knew he would stop at nothing to make her his. She ended the words of the song on a breathy whisper that had his hard-on aching to be freed. This woman was passion in the flesh. His need for her was approaching dangerous levels.

After she sang a half dozen or more standards, she leaned toward the microphone and said, "I've got to take a small break. Please head to the bar to purchase CDs, pins, posters, T-shirts. As always, the proceeds benefit the Southeast Louisiana Autism Society. Thank you."

Autism? She was a philanthropist. That surely wasn't on Camp's list of reasons she moonlighted as a lounge singer, and he wondered why she chose that cause to support. She certainly wasn't plagued with autism. One of Mandy's cousins had had autism. He'd line up objects: pens, pencils, tacks, quarters, Q-tips. He always kept his head down too, since he could never look anyone in the eye.

Fifteen minutes later, Jenny returned to the stage with a guitar player.

The second half of her set started with "Besame Mucho." Jenny stood center stage at the microphone, clutching the stand in her fingertips as her head tilted to one side. She closed her eyes and swayed ever so slightly with the light sounds of the guitar.

Camp, sitting at that table in a little lounge in the French Quarter of New Orleans, fell in love for the first time in his life. All those times he'd thought he was in love were just a stretch before the marathon of emotion now coursing through his veins.

When she was done, Camp waited for her to come out from backstage. When she did, she'd changed into jeans and one of the Autism Society T-shirts. The young guitar player followed her around like a puppy. Camp suspected he was younger than Jenny, but he was a lot bigger, and that bothered him. She was busy gathering up her paraphernalia, the guitar player helping her, using the opportunity to touch her whenever possible, and Camp's blood was simmering in his veins. He walked up behind them, and she turned too quickly, exhaling a shocked gasp when they bumped.

"Oh!" She laid her hand on her chest to catch her breath. "Camp, you startled me."

He looked at her—at her face, into her eyes—and at that moment no one else existed. He was alone in the bar with her.

"You are beautiful, and my God, when you sing, you are celestial."

He pulled her to him and kissed her sweetly and thoroughly. When they pulled apart, she had to catch her breath.

"How did you . . . " Her face wore confusion. "What are you doing here?"

"Does it upset you that I'm here?" Camp looked away, suddenly unsure. Just because he'd had an epiphany didn't mean that she felt the same way.

She cradled his cheeks with her palms, drawing his eyes back to her face.

"No, Camp, it doesn't upset me. I'm rather glad to see you." She kissed him on the nose.

Grasping her hands and pulling her in close and tight, he asked, "Can I take you home, then?"

With desire flaring in her gaze, she smiled and nodded. "Please."

"She came with me." Guitar boy's words interrupted their little cocoon.

"Sorry, dude. Looks like you'll be flying solo."

***

As Camp drove, he was overcome with the feelings he had for Jenny. He knew his family would tease. He always fell hard and fast, but what he realized tonight was that he'd never loved any of the women before her.

She'd told him she was free for the night and had then fallen asleep against his shoulder. He loved how the weight of her felt against him and the thought of her being so comfortable with him that she could just drift off, but he'd noted that she was constantly exhausted and it worried him.

Jenny gripped his arm tight in her delicate hands. She was talking in her sleep and so he lowered the volume on the CD that he'd purchased. She'd laughed when he turned it on.

"Andrew. Where are you, Andrew?"

Andrew? Her son? He'd heard her on the phone with him. When had she had a baby? Was there a father in the picture? His sense of possession was growing stronger by the minute. His plan for the night was to take her to his family's estate in Whiskey Cove. He didn't want to risk being interrupted at his house by Cash or Isa or anyone else. He'd confided in Clay and been instructed on the ever so delicate art of orgasm denial, and since his father had taken the horses out of state to show, he planned to use the stables for his first foray into what Clay called the dark side.

He could admit to himself in the darkness of the car that just touching Jenny, loving her, would probably be enough.

Yeah, he wanted to tease her, get her to open up to him and answer his questions, but he wanted to please her. Please himself by getting lost inside her body. Still, he didn't intend his planning to go to waste. Just thinking of the ways he'd drive Jenny crazy had had him hard for hours.

When he pulled up to the stables, Jenny was still asleep, so he carried her in and laid her on the bed he'd fashioned out of hay and blankets. He'd earlier brought down pillows from the house and placed those around the bed as well. He'd chosen a rather narrow stall where the walls were already outfitted with hooks that he could use to secure her to the bed, leaving his hands free to love her body to distraction.

Jenny was always tired, exhausted really, and now Camp understood why. But that worked to his advantage tonight. He began to slowly undress her, his worry for her coming to the fore. Her focus seemed like it wasn't always with her on the job site, like she'd left it somewhere else. He wondered why she was always tired—was it simply the two jobs? Andrew? Or was there something else, something he could help her with? He'd asked her countless times, but she never shared. Tonight he'd get the answers he sought.

She stirred and opened her eyes, looking up and around at the high ceilings of the stable. She inhaled deeply. "Horses." She smiled just a bit. Then her hand patted the flannel atop the bed. With hooded eyes she asked, "What's going on?"

"We're in the stables on my father's land. I want to restrain you with these silk scarves." He slowly laced the scarves through his fingers so she could see them. Her throat engaged as she swallowed, and her mouth opened on a breathy exhale. She eyed the crop hanging next to the head of the bed. She lifted it and snapped it through the air. "Will you be using this?"

His mouth went dry. "Do you want me to?"

She licked her lips as she lowered her head, and then she peeked up at him with a coy, wide-eyed smile. "Maybe."

She was responding to his setup like a pro, but he couldn't figure her out. He'd been prepared to have to convince her to play.

"Have you done this before?" he asked.

"What? The crop, the silk ties?" She looked at the scarves in his hands and smiled. "No, but I can't say I haven't thought about being restrained and at your mercy."

Holy fuck! This woman had been made just for him. Images of her naked and restrained had him seeing stars. He swallowed hard. "When were you thinking about it?"

"Any time you run around spouting off orders to the contractors and everyone else in the vicinity. You're always so commanding, it turns me on." Her lust-filled eyes bored into him.

I'm commanding? Well, if that isn't the pot calling the kettle black. She'd pay for that. He placed his palm on her cheek and finished undressing her. Once he had her stripped down to her cream-colored silk thong panties, he knotted the multi-colored silk scarves around her wrists and ankles. He whispered of her beauty in her ear and massaged her shoulders as he tied her off. With the scarves tied to her, he laced each one through the metal eyehooks in the boards, attaching her loosely.

When he had her secured, he stood back and took in her bound form. Her nipples hardened even as he watched.

"Mmm, Camp."

He picked up the riding crop and snapped it against the bed. Her body tensed as she tested the silk restraints. Seeing the desire in her eyes, he slowly unbuttoned his shirt. Her gaze never left him. As he slid the shirt down his arms, she swiped her tongue across her bottom lip. He left his snug black trousers on and lay alongside her.

Her nipples hardened even more under his gaze, and he took one into his mouth and rolled it between his teeth. Using the crop on the other breast, he delivered light taps that had her bowing her back. He bit lightly, and her tongue darted out to wet her lips. She groaned low in the back of her throat. He massaged lightly between her legs, over the material of her panties. As her body arched, her limbs pulled the scarves tight and her eyes closed. He slid his hand beneath the fabric of her panties and discovered she was already extremely wet. He could feel how close she was when his thumb rubbed the hard knot at the top of her thighs.

"I'm going to come, don't stop." She panted.

Camp pulled his hand away and stood. Her eyes flew open and when she settled her gaze on him, her stare narrowed and she pierced him with those liquid chocolate pupils. He maneuvered out of her reach; he didn't want to be kicked or punched if she freed herself, which she could do since he hadn't tied the scarves tightly. He held the riding crop in his hand, dangling it at his side. He grinned at her, knowing she'd figured out his plan.

He lowered himself between her legs and kissed her inner thigh. Parting his lips, he applied light suction to her skin and used the bristles from his day-old beard to rub across the apex of her thighs, across her cloth-covered pussy. He moved to her other thigh and repeated the same series of actions. He opened his mouth, using his hot breath to whisper across her skin and the wetness at her crotch. She started to buck and mewl. Camp had her right where he wanted her. He slid his tongue across the spot of moisture on her panties. He passed through it once more and then sucked on the material gently.

She spread her legs open as far as the bonds would let her. On an exaggerated moan she said his name, and he pressed in with his tongue at the cloth-covered juncture between her thighs. Her panties were practically translucent, and the thin strip of material didn't cover much of anything but her seam. She moved her hips to grind against his tongue, but he grabbed her and pinned her down. She let out a strangled cry. He slowly pulled the wet strip of material aside and exposed her glistening cunt to the crisp night air that further teased her moistened channel. Using his fingers, Camp pulled the outer lips of her sex apart and waited. He watched as her muscles contracted in frustration. She was utterly helpless. Her core was dripping and as he sat watching, more of her moisture leaked from within. It was fascinating.

"Camp!"

Her entire body convulsed as she screamed. He repositioned his fingers, using them to massage her. He sucked and pinched with his lips.

God, she tasted good. He started to tremble.

Another choked-off moan escaped her lips. "Camp please." The raspy whisper just reached his ears.

"Please what?"

"Please finish me."

"Are you ready to come?"

"Yeeeeees!"

"First tell me why you won't give me a chance." Camp sucked lightly at her flesh.

"What chance?"

"A chance to be with you. A chance to get to know you."

"I can't," Jenny cried.

Using his tongue, he laved painfully slow at her opening to just below her clit and back down. "Who is Andrew?" he whispered against her slit.

Huffing, and squirming, she replied, "My brother."

Camp kept up his attention between her legs. "Why doesn't your mother take care of him?"

She lifted her shoulders from the bed and attempted to bring her thighs together to fight the need he'd pushed her into. He doubled his efforts, licking ever so slightly up and down her crease while using his fingers to massage just the outer lips. He knew his touch was too light to set her free.

"Camp, please."

"Do you want me to stop?"

"No!"

"If you answer my questions, I'll take care of you. That's the deal." He spoke against her thighs so she could feel the sensation made by the vibrations of his mouth. "Why does your mother not take care of Andrew?"

"Ugh!"

"If you don't answer, I untie you and let you take care of yourself. The choice is yours."

"Because she"—Jenny gasped and writhed—"because she can't."

"Why?" Camp used the crop to lightly slap her swollen flesh.

Jenny cried out. "She's dead. My mother is dead."

Camp was stunned. Her mother had died? Somewhat recently, depending on how old the child was. Given the conversation he'd heard, he would guess no more than five years.

"Camp, please."

Jenny's plea got through to him. He wasn't quite done with his questions, but he needed to hold her so that meant he needed to release her. She didn't protest. When she was free, she climbed on top of him, straddled his thighs, and slowly lowered herself onto his erection. She rode him slow and steady at first, then she became erratic and frenzied. She kept going until she wasn't able to keep the pace and collapsed on his chest and started to sob. Sobs turned into moans, moans turned into wails. She beat at his chest with closed fists.

All the while Camp just took it from her. She'd been angry when he'd met her. Clay had told him there was something burning inside her, said he'd seen it time and again at the club. Women went in to be dominated and taken to a place free from all their problems.

Jenny's wrath eventually burned out. When she was weak and exhausted, she lay down next to him and curled into his side.

"Jenny, what are you angry about?"

"I'm angry because I don't get to live the life I want."

Bingo. He turned into Jenny so that they were facing each other on their sides. "Why can't you have the life you want?"

"I have my autistic brother to take care of for the rest of my life."

Well, damn. That was certainly a reason to be angry. She was Andrew's provider *and* caregiver. And he was the one with autism. That was a lot for anyone to take on, especially a sibling.

And autism must have its challenges. He thought of Mandy's cousin and how it would not do to leave him unsupervised. One night he'd gotten out of bed and took off on foot in the direction of "the beam in the sky." It had turned out to be a spotlight at a car dealership. He'd been picked up by the police for trying to cross the interstate on foot. Now that he was older, however, he was in some kind of vocational day program.

"Maybe when he's older he can get a job."

Jenny sat up and wiped at her eyes. "He's seventeen now. I don't think it's going to happen."

He followed her into a sitting position. "He's seventeen? When did your mom die? And where's your dad?"

She blew out a long breath. "Nine years ago, I was eighteen and in the air force, attending the center for professional development. I was training to be a defense finance manager. My parents died in a fire. Andrew got out, but they didn't make it. I left the air force to care for Andrew."

Damn. So she'd lost both parents and her future. Andrew would have been about eight at the time.

"Where are my clothes? I need you to take me home."

"You said you were free for the night and we're not done."

"I need to go."

"We're not done."

Jenny looked up into Camp's eyes. "I can't accommodate you right now."

"I don't need accommodating."

"Well, what the hell do you want?"

Camp pushed a strand of hair behind her ear. "I want to be with you, day and night."

She shook her head. "My nights belong to Andrew."

Camp pulled her into his chest and wrapped his legs around her. "All right, then. I want to be with you and Andrew." He kissed her cheek. "I need to be with you."

And she needed him.

She just couldn't see it.

CHAPTER 6

Jenny was singing as she idly folded laundry. She seemed to be singing a lot more lately. She knew it had to do with how things had been going with Camp, once he'd finally gotten past her defenses. She'd wanted to say yes when he'd asked her out so many times before, but Andrew required all of her extra time and she'd not thought it fair to subject another person to her endless problems.

Jenny had been delighted to see Camp at the lounge. As far as she knew, she'd never performed for friends or coworkers. She wondered how he knew she'd be there, but he seemed dead set on keeping that to himself. His words after she'd finished her set had meant everything. Had he really said, *You are beautiful, and my God, when you sing, you are celestial?* She never wanted to forget that—*celestial*. Then he'd taken her back to his childhood home and extracted her secrets, secrets she didn't even want to face herself. Lord, how he'd looked standing at the end of the bed, his gaze intense on her and the riding crop loose in his hands. He'd looked dangerous. And powerful. And hot.

His tight trousers had hung low on his taut, muscled, and veined body. He'd burned in his intensity, and his eyes had become a vortex in a storm. That night she actually thought it might be possible to catch fire. The ignition point would have been her burning sex. It was burning for him now.

She'd finally agreed to let Camp meet Andrew. She'd done it before. But only a couple of times. He'd met Richard. But that hadn't turned out well for any of them.

She'd met Richard when she was in the air force. Three years later, they'd maintained their relationship long distance while he was overseas. When he returned, Jenny had been twenty-one and very much in love. But Andrew hated Richard. They'd tried to introduce Andrew to the idea of becoming a family and slowly Richard had started coming around more, but Andrew had become increasingly more aggressive toward him. One morning Richard went out to his car to find that Andrew had taken a hammer to it. It had been so bad his insurance company declared the car a total loss. Andrew had been only eleven. Jenny couldn't expect Richard to stay around after that.

She'd already decided that if Andrew didn't warm to Camp, she'd have to let him go, but her mind couldn't zero in on what to do if Andrew were to like Camp. Where would they be then? It was probably nothing to worry about because she was ninety-nine percent sure Andrew would never warm to any man.

***

Camp was running a brush through his hair. He'd just showered and was about to go downstairs to make sure everything was just as he wanted it. It had taken several weeks for Camp to talk Jenny into letting him meet Andrew. Today was the day.

When Camp found out Andrew loved horses, he contacted his father. Jenny had told him she was worried about Andrew becoming aggressive toward him. Evidently that was how her brother dealt with the men in her life, and dealing with the drama and trauma had taken a toll on Jenny. As Camp understood it, that was why she'd decided she couldn't ever be with anyone.

He was going to make it his mission to bond with the kid. And he'd begin with horses.

At Camp's request, his father had acquired a relatively young Missouri fox trotter. He'd told his father that above all else, it was imperative the horse be gentle. He'd worked with the breed before, and they'd all been gentle and calm. Dreamer was no different; she would go anywhere he pointed her head. Still, Camp was a little worried because while Andrew loved horses, he'd never ridden one. Camp had been working with the horse daily, relieved that neither yapping dogs nor racing rabbits bothered Dreamer's calm demeanor. She didn't spook easily and had even remained calm around a backfiring car.

Today was the day he'd meet Andrew. He and Jenny were headed to the estate right now.

Camp had done his research, and at first he'd been overwhelmed. There was a wealth of information about autism that had left him frustrated. After reading for hours he'd come to the conclusion that nobody had answers. He'd come up with his own plan since it wouldn't do to have Andrew getting hurt. He planned to be consistent and make his expectations clear.

He'd put together a checklist of tasks that needed to take place before Andrew could ride. Jenny had told him that lists were an important part of Andrew's daily routine and that without them he was lost. Camp guessed such structure could work to his advantage. After all, he was a planner and a lists kind of guy too.

When they pulled onto the estate, Camp was standing on the front porch. As soon as the car was parked, Andrew jumped out and inquired about the horse.

Jenny was explaining to Andrew that he wouldn't be riding today. Camp had told her to make sure he was clear on that point.

She asked, "Andrew, what are you doing with the horse today?"

Andrew rocked on one leg and held his gaze to the ground. "Grooming."

"That's right, grooming."

Camp walked up to them. He wanted to embrace Jenny, but he needed Andrew to accept him first, so he just nodded to her. She seemed timid when she nodded back.

Jenny placed her hand on Andrew's upper arm. "Andrew, this is Camp."

He looked up at Camp's shoulder. "Camp has a horse named Dreamer."

Camp nodded. "That's right. I understand you like horses."

Andrew said, "Yes. And dogs." He resumed his rocking behavior. "Andrew has to learn the rules first."

"There are a few rules to learn for your safety and the safety of the horse."

Andrew flapped his hands and asked, "What are the rules?"

"Let's go into the house and I'll show you."

Andrew, with nut-brown hair and chocolate eyes, favored Jenny. His voice was low, and he had the same copper highlights in his hair that were so alluring on her.

Andrew and Jenny followed him into the large home. He took them to the kitchen where a poster board rested against one wall.

Andrew read, "Meeting Dreamer for the first time."

Camp said, "That's right, keep reading." Camp had numbered each bullet point, but he covered all but the first with paper so he could control the pace and ensure that Andrew truly understood.

"When meeting a horse for the first time, always stay toward the front, left of the horse."

Camp clarified, "*Always* front left. If you stand at the back, the horse might kick you hard."

Camp exposed the second rule.

They read through each rule in the same manner, Camp always following up to confirm Andrew understood the rule. When they finished, Camp took Andrew to meet Dreamer.

Camp told Andrew to wait until he gave him the all clear signal to come into the ring and approach Dreamer. He stood with Jenny against the fence and waited.

"Okay, Andrew," Camp waved him in.

Andrew walked in a calm but deliberate manner just as Camp had instructed. He stood to the front left of the horse and extended the back of his hand to her nose. Dreamer sniffed his hand and snorted. Then she rubbed her cheek on Andrew's hand. Andrew called her by name several times and exhaled near the horse's nose, going through the rules step by step. Camp handed him a curry comb, and Andrew massaged down the left side of the horse as Camp instructed.

Jenny stood at the fence and watched; occasionally she'd give a wave. He hoped she was pleased with how things were going.

He was beginning to understand the boy. Andrew was like a horse—he startled easily and was very cautious. He needed clear and deliberate instruction. Camp imagined that if Andrew could live in this bubble on the estate, protected by boundaries, he would probably be just fine, but life wouldn't allow that. There would always be intrusions from the outside world. And life, as it inevitably did, would remind him that he wasn't immune in his bubble. That same thing had happened to Camp when he was a teenager. His prized Tennessee walker, Noah, had died abruptly. The death had been hard on Camp. The memory of his loss had him wondering how Andrew had processed his parents' deaths.

Just as Andrew was building trust with Dreamer, Camp was doing so with Andrew. When Camp walked Jenny and Andrew to their car, he asked if he could join them for dinner at their home. Andrew answered, "On Saturday we order pizza, and I play online computer games."

To clarify, Camp asked, "Andrew, can I join you for pizza and hang out with your sister while you play games?"

"Yes."

Camp shrugged and with wide eyes looked to Jenny.

Jenny smiled at him. "Seven o'clock?"

"I'll be there."

Andrew lifted his hand and offered Camp an awkward wave. "Bye. Thanks for letting me meet Dreamer."

**

After pizza, Andrew retreated to his room to play on the computer. Jenny cleared her throat and said to Camp, "He'll be in there the rest of the night."

Camp was relieved because he needed to drop a bomb on Jenny and he needed her to seriously consider his life-changing proposal. "Where's your bedroom?"

He had a plan and for what he had to tell, he needed her frustrated, writhing, and on the brink of climax, or there would be no way she'd agree.

Once her bedroom door was closed, Jenny turned and pulled his hair hard as she slammed their mouths together and took what she needed. He roughly undressed her, removing her pants and ripping the buttons on her blouse, jerking it down her arms. Her hands were trapped in the shirt, and he used her inability to free herself to pull her arms behind her and push her down to the bed.

"Can you keep quiet, Jenny, or shall I gag you?"

Her voice was breathy—aroused and arousing—when she said, "Andrew wears earphones, but I'll try to be quiet."

"Good girl." He used his open palm to smack her right ass cheek.

Over the past few weeks they'd fought and talked and fought some more. He understood her more now. She considered Andrew her burden and didn't want to impose on Camp. She'd said her greatest fear was that she'd wake one day and he'd regret ever having met her. That saddened him at first, but then he became angry that she would think that of him. Given her past he understood and he let it go.

She'd said she didn't feel in control of her life or her future. That helped him understand why Jenny liked rough, angry sex—it was an outlet for her frustration—If that was how she needed it, he'd comply, but he hoped one day she'd appreciate slow, sensual fucking too. He loved it rough as much as she did, but sometimes he needed to connect with her in an atmosphere other than one painted with anger. When she was sleepy and sated she was open to tenderness, but that was the only time she'd permit him to love her gently. And even that was tricky. She didn't like making herself vulnerable, and being able to bolt home was an easy out for her. He'd asked her repeatedly to move to the ranch so they could all live there together, but she continually refused.

Once he was naked, he sat next to her as she lay helpless and face down on the bed. He pulled her to her side, her back to his front, and slid his arm over her hip and around to the front of her body, tracing down her abdomen and between her legs to massage her sex. With his other hand he pumped into her with two fingers from behind until she was softly mewling.

When he had her at the point of climax, he balanced her there and told her what he'd been working up to for the past few days.

"Jenny, I want you and Andrew to move in with me. We'll live at the estate. I've already cleared it with my father, and I've contacted a sitter as well. She has twenty years' experience working with special needs individuals."

"What?" She was panting, but she'd stilled at his first words.

"I think you heard what I said."

She twisted her body to escape his hold, but he held her in position.

"Let me go, Camp."

"Not this time."

He tapped her directly on her clit. She moaned. He picked up the massage where he'd left off.

"I want to be with you. It makes perfect sense. I can help you with Andrew."

Her voice faint, she said, "Camp, what happens when you've had enough? You can walk away, but I can't ever walk away. What guarantees will I have that you won't walk out? You walked out on your wife. And didn't you break it off with your fiancée too? Was she not meeting your expectations? You're so demanding and you expect everyone around you to be perfect. Andrew and I are far from perfect."

Now he was pissed. And how did she know about Kim? The local papers he guessed. Hell, they were probably all Facebook friends. He stood to avoid doing something he'd regret and instead paced the room. She sat up, wrestled her arms back into her shirt, and pulled her knees to her chest. He ran his fingers through his short hair.

"Where is this coming from? Have I ever made you feel inferior, that you were less than perfect?"

God, had he been a prick without knowing it? He thought she was perfect—hadn't he made that clear the last few weeks?

Her voice steady, she said, "Do I count the time you told me I was fucking useless?"

He stopped pacing. His eyes narrowed at her, and he cocked his head. She was staring at his fully erect dick as she made her way to the end of the bed on her knees. She grasped his cock and began to stroke him with her warm hands. He pulled away.

"That's bullshit! Tell me why you don't want me."

She sat back on her heels and dropped her head. "I never said that. I want you, sometimes so badly I can't even think straight, but I can't let myself give in to that emotion, that desire." Her voice was low, defeated. "It would be easy for me to let you do everything, but then where would I be when you decided to leave us?"

He stepped forward and grasped her hands in his. "I swear to you it wouldn't be that way."

Her head shook with ferocity. She whispered, "You can't make promises like that, Camp. No one can."

He clasped her cheek in his hand and tried to think like her.

She'd been through so much already, including relationships with men who no doubt thought they could deal with Andrew if doing so meant they would have Jenny and all her sex and beauty. But there was much more to love than that, to being together and creating a family, and the negative aspects had outweighed the positives and they'd bolted.

"You're right; no one can promise forever. But if you marry me, you become part of my family. It would give you the insurance you need and if anything were to happen to me, you would have any number of people willing to help you, willing to call you family, loving you and Andrew unconditionally."

She was as still as a wooden statue as she stared off into the distance.

Camp bent and gently kissed her lips. "Jenny, I love you. Marry me."

Her breath escaped on a gasp as her hands reached up to cup his cheek. "Camp, I think I love you too, but I'm not ready to marry you. I don't know if I will ever be. Can you be okay with that? I know how you get when you want something, and I'm not convinced you'll just let us be as we are, no more marriage talk." She ran a thumb across his lower lip. "But that's all I can do right now. Can you accept that?"

No, he wouldn't be able to not constantly think of making her take his name, but he'd hold that information close to his chest.

"I can if it means keeping your love."

But she'd marry him eventually, by God. Even if he had to force her. And she wouldn't be able to claim that she didn't expect that of him.

Yeah, he'd come to know her, understand her. But she knew him as well. She'd never be able to pretend that she didn't expect him to try to get his way by any means necessary.

CHAPTER 7

Jenny sat on the porch sipping hot tea and reading a book. Something she hadn't been able to do in a while—just be—no responsibilities, no next meal to prepare, no clothes to wash. Jenny had put her trust in Camp. She trusted him when he said, which he often did, that they would build a life together. That they would find their way and that Andrew was part of it. She'd thought he was crazy when he'd asked her to marry him, but she'd agreed to move to his family estate and see how things went. Plus Andrew had made it clear a few weeks ago that he wanted to be closer to Camp when he'd abruptly packed up his belongings and told her he was leaving to go live with Camp.

She had been beside herself with joy that Andrew actually wanted to include Camp, so much so that he wanted to leave the safety of his own home. She hadn't had to talk him into anything. It was almost the reverse with Camp and Andrew trying to convince her moving to the estate was a good idea.

They decided to keep the home she had in Baton Rouge; she wasn't ready to let it go. That had been a bit of an issue because Camp thought she was keeping it in case things with him didn't work out. He'd tied her facedown to their bed until she swore to him that above all else, she did trust him when he said they would be together forever. Thinking back on that afternoon had her thighs moistening with need for him. She loved how he took what he wanted and gave exactly what she needed.

They moved into the large estate and let Andrew fix his room to his liking. He did a rodeo theme. Jenny didn't know where he'd picked up an interest in rodeo, but he followed professional bull riders, horse riders, and barrel racers. Everything. The estate seemed to agree with Andrew. Cory

42

and Brook even gave him a yellow lab puppy. To Jenny's astonishment, Andrew was independently caring for the dog. Camp had posted a daily-dog-duties checklist, and Andrew followed it to the letter. Camp had told him that if he didn't follow the list, the dog would have to go live with Cory and Brook, who would follow the rules.

It seemed Campbell St. Martin had a knack for working with Andrew, and it was clear Andrew loved Camp. His eyes would follow him across the room or the yard, wherever he went. Andrew was always asking Camp where he was going, so Camp had taken to announcing his plans even if he was just going to the bathroom. His accommodations for Andrew made Jenny laugh.

Andrew had even picked up some of Camp's bad habits, like eating Oreo cookies for breakfast. The sitter had been working out too. She was very patient with Andrew. Since Andrew was seventeen, Camp advised her to supervise him while letting his independence flourish. Jenny had laughed at that. Here she'd just been trying to survive, tread water, and Camp had an entire philosophy for dealing with her brother.

Eventually Camp's father came home, and Andrew took to him as well. He'd said to Jenny, "There's two of them." She'd only nodded, wondering what he'd say when he met Cash.

Camp had wanted to introduce his large family slowly so Andrew wasn't overwhelmed.

Instead Jenny was the one overwhelmed. By Camp's generosity and patience and tenderness.

***

They'd all been together at the estate for six weeks. It was Saturday morning and Jenny was feeling particularly overjoyed at how well the transitions in her life had played out. She stretched deep and long, not ready to leave the warm soft cocoon she shared with Camp, who was still asleep. She couldn't believe how good Camp was with Andrew. He was better with him than all the therapists combined. He seemed to understand Andrew's need for rules and clear expectations. She knew from working with Camp that he was overly particular about organization and lists and schedule systems. That had always been hard for her since she wasn't a planner, but Andrew had forced her to plan things out. And Andrew had taken to Camp like a child with a new puppy. She was amazed whenever she watched them together, especially each time Andrew did something he'd never done. Like the day he hugged Camp.

Her heart had overflowed with joy when Andrew wrapped his arms around Camp. Camp had smiled and hugged him back, and then the two of them had continued with their task—washing Camp's truck—with nothing else said. Jenny had fought off happy tears for hours.

She knew she loved Camp, and she'd tried to tell him several times. He didn't seem to have any problem getting the words out and was always telling her how much she meant to him.

"Camp?"

He slowly came to at her words. He grabbed at his morning hard-on and let out a long satisfied groan. "Come ride me."

Jenny complied and climbed across his lap.

"Turn around," Camp commanded.

He loved watching her take him in that position. As she turned, her sex rubbed his cock and once she was in place, she leaned forward on her hands, exposing herself to Camp. He held his cock in his hands until her warmth fully swallowed his erection. She took him so slowly it was painful.

It must have been painful, the good kind of painful, for Camp too. He groaned as she took the final inch of him.

Jenny knew how he liked it. Once his penis opened her channel enough, she leaned forward and arched her ass up by placing her chest closer to his legs. Camp was visual, and every time she arched up, he moaned. She liked to look back at him as he watched, his focus intense, where their bodies connected.

"Ride my cock with your tight little cunt."

She started rocking down and back. He groaned out expletives.

"God, I can see you, feel you, gripping me like a fist."

She arched herself into a wave motion and repeatedly slid up and down. He would let her lead for a while, but he always ended up taking over. This morning was no exception. Jenny loved his dominance and when he grasped her hips and held her in place while he pistoned hard and fast into her, she became lost in his consumption.

When he released her hips, she resumed her wave motion. She knew what was about to happen when he ran his middle finger through their moisture. He massaged the ring of muscle at her ass and inserted his finger slowly, all the way. While she rode him, he turned the finger inside her and pulled it out to the first knuckle and then thrust it back in harder.

"Are you going to come?"

"Yes."

"Touch yourself, let me hear you."

As she came she told him, "I love you more than you could ever know."

He turned them until he was on top. He kissed her forehead, each of her eyes, her nose, and to the side of each of her lips. He smiled down at her as he whispered, "I've waited a lifetime to hear you say that. Tell me again."

"I love you."

He held her face, his eyes never leaving hers, as he loved her tenderly.

And he held her when she sobbed out her release.

Then she held him while he drew word pictures of how wonderful their life was going to be.

After she declared her love, the days ran together. Life on the estate was great. Too great, Jenny thought. Since when had her life ever run like clockwork? She knew the answer—since she had submitted to Camp.

With an autistic brother, Jenny had always been on alert. So she expected something to happen. Something always did. Things could go from calm to chaotic in a matter of seconds. But she was learning to rely on Camp. He'd promised to share some of the burden, and she'd promised to let him.

But with Andrew, there was no way to know what would trigger the chaos. However, on one particular day she knew to be on high alert. It was the anniversary of their parents' deaths and every year, Andrew had been aware of the date. Around seven in the morning, Jenny left Camp asleep in their bed and went to check in with her brother. She wanted to confirm he was dealing with the significance of this day in a healthy manner and to let him know that if he wanted smiley-face pancakes, she would make them. It was high time he gave up the Oreo fetish.

When she opened the door to his room, he wasn't there. She checked the bathroom, but he wasn't there either. She frantically started opening all the doors along the hallway and calling out his name.

***

When Camp heard the alarm in Jenny's voice, he was up in a flash. He grabbed a pair of jeans and ran to the sound of her voice.

"Camp! I can't find Andrew."

He took the stairs three at a time. He searched the kitchen, living areas, den, dining room, and solarium. From the enclosed glass solarium at the back of the main house, he saw that the stable door was ajar. He knew he had latched it last night, and no one else would have left it open.

Camp hurriedly made his way to the stables. He called for Andrew, but it was no use. Dreamer was gone. He did a quick search and saw the saddle and helmet on the wall. Maybe Andrew was simply walking the horse. Camp jumped on an all terrain vehicle and set in search of the horse and boy. They weren't in the paddock and Camp thought Andrew must be riding the horse. That would not be good. Andrew had only ever sat the horse in the paddock in full dress and with Camp leading.

Camp drove far out on the property and was about to head back when he saw Dreamer. The horse was on the other side of the fence, indicating that Andrew must have jumped the horse. Camp screamed Andrew's name as loud as he could. He jumped from the ATV and searched the field. High grasses and bushes compromised his vision. He strode toward Dreamer and saw something dark against the green of the grass. Nut-brown hair.

He ran to Andrew, finding him unconscious. He didn't move him in case his neck or back had been injured. There was blood near his head and on a nearby rock. Andrew's head had landed on the rock.

"Andrew?" He called loudly, but Andrew didn't move. Camp, hands shaking, checked his pulse. It was steady. His chest was rising and falling. "Andrew?"

His father's truck was driving across the field. It stopped and his father and Jenny ran toward him. When Jenny saw her brother she went down on her knees and screamed his name. His dad was already talking to emergency services.

Camp eyed Jenny, who was sitting in the grass, stroking her brother's hand and whispering, "I caused this."

A shiver raced through Camp. Like Andrew, she didn't move when he dropped next to her. She just whispered again, "I caused this."

CHAPTER 8

Camp was towing Jenny through the hospital corridor behind Andrew's gurney. He felt the halt in their progression the moment she froze in place.

"Jenny?" He gently tugged her forward, but she fought and escaped his grip. "Baby?" She was shaking her head. He drew her tightly into his chest. "Jenny, I'm here. Nothing matters right now but helping Andrew. No matter what happens, know in your heart I'll be here to help you through it."

They followed Andrew into the bowels of the hospital until they finally stopped at a door with a biohazard sign. They were shown into a small office and asked to wait there for the nurse.

Jenny was nonresponsive, so Camp spoke with the nurse, doctor, and a social worker. He related exactly what had happened. He was speaking with the social worker when she pointed to Jenny and said she didn't think she, Jenny, was capable of caring for Andrew's needs. Then the woman grilled him hard about the responsibilities of parents with special needs kids.

She went on and on until Camp wanted to throttle the woman. Had that been what it was like for Jenny since she'd been eighteen, everyone judging her when they had no idea what it was like to raise a child with autism? God, she'd taken on a little brother and his autism when she'd been a kid herself. The nerve of this woman to judge her.

After he'd had enough, been polite for much longer than the social worker deserved, Camp took control. He stood. "Let me ask you a question, Mrs. Daily. Do you have a child with autism?"

She responded tersely. "No, I do not."

"How about a kid with a special need?"

Camp could tell she was getting pissed. Good—he didn't want to be the only one. Her lips tight, she said, "No."

"So you shouldn't sit there in judgment of those that do. It's hard.

47

Damned hard. Your job is not to make life any harder for those who have to care for those unable to care for themselves. In fact, your job is probably to collect the facts, leaving your personal thoughts to yourself. If you want to accuse us of being irresponsible, then do it in a court of law. If not, then let us get back to my family."

Jenny's head turned in his direction, and her wide eyes were filled with tears when she mouthed his name, but no sound emerged.

He pulled her up by the hand. "Come on, baby. Let's get back to focusing on Andrew."

In the waiting area, Clay's family had trickled in until they were all present in support of him and Jenny and Andrew. He was worried about Jenny. Andrew was getting the care he needed—Camp couldn't do anything else for him. But Jenny . . . He had to be able to do something for her.

She didn't speak, just stared ahead with glassy eyes. A doctor came out to speak with them and she still didn't acknowledge that she heard anything.

It was good news; Andrew had moved from severe to minor on the coma scale. He was coming around slowly, and whatever they'd done to release the pressure in his skull had worked. Brain scans showed no residual damage.

Camp turned to Jenny and lifted her head. "Hey, did you hear that? Andrew's going to be okay." She blinked at him and gasped as she collapsed into his arms.

***

That night Camp anticipated all of Jenny's needs. He fed her grilled cheese and tomato soup. He ran a wet towel over her face and combed her hair. He removed their clothes and pulled her in close to spoon her in bed. Camp tenderly kneaded her breast and skimmed his fingers delicately down to her abdomen. His touch remained gentle. He wanted to love her, wanted her to know that she was okay, that Andrew was going to be fine. His penis slid between the wetness at her thighs. She started to fight him, turning to position herself on top.

"No, Jenny, let me love you."

He traced a loose hair back behind her ear and cupped her face in his palm. His touch remained soft as he trailed the pads of his fingers over her breasts and down her arms. When Jenny tried to grind on him, he said, "Not tonight, baby. Let go and let me show you how much I love you."

Tonight he would take care of her, love her unconditionally. Tonight he would give, would begin to fill up the empty places that had been drained from years of giving and giving and giving.

Jenny gripped and squeezed him hard in her hand, positioning him at her entrance. "But I need it hard and rough."

Camp spooned her again while at the same time letting his fingers slide sensually down her thigh, over her hips and down to the front of her sex. He massaged her softly. "You need it like this too."

"No, I need to feel the pain." She bucked her ass hard against his groin.

He whispered, "No, Jenny, you need to feel loved."

He held her close and slid his firmness into her from behind. The hand at the front of her sex massaged her delicately to climax.

They made love into the night. At some point Camp sat on the edge of the bed and stood Jenny, with her back to him, between his legs. She placed her hands on his thighs and arched her back. He held her throat, tilting her head back to rest on his shoulder. Her chest bowed out. With his fee hand Camp rubbed his shaft through the slick lips of her pussy and pushed in steadily. Jenny was taking it slow now. As much as Camp loved her animalistic behavior in bed, he was in awe at this new Jenny. She rocked slowly back and forth on his cock in a leisurely erotic dance that, coupled with her moaning, had him shattering around her within minutes. When she turned around to lower him to the bed, her eyes smoldered with desire. She was a glowing cinder as she rode him, seeking her release.

***

The next morning Jenny left Camp in their bed at the estate and drove to a place that held the memories of her past. She stood in front of the remnants of the farmhouse where she grew up. She recalled running in the tall grass, chasing butterflies with a net. She stepped on something hard and looked down to see the now rusty metal pan she had used to feed the stray cats. Her mother had caught her sneaking food out to the cats and told her that if she didn't stop feeding them, every cat in town would be in their yard. Jenny had hoped for that and kept feeding them.

She walked around to the backyard. The old swing set mimicked a frown with its saggy plastic seat and broken chains. The rusty old slide had warped. She saw the spot where Andrew had passed countless hours at the tire swing under the pecan tree. Jenny walked over to it, tested the strength of the rope, and climbed into the tire. She sat on the swing and thought about what she had set into motion so many years ago.

Fate was a powerful force. An inescapable one.

Jenny remembered when her parents died and the news sank in that she would be the sole guardian of her autistic brother. She was eighteen and had horrible thoughts about how she could be set free. She'd hated her brother back then and wanted to leave so many times. Had wanted to get out and just run. Had wanted to be free of the responsibilities. Free of the bonds. Free of . . . She squeezed her eyes closed, but the words had already sprung to life. She had wanted to be free of Andrew.

She sat in the tire swing and rocked until her body was numb.

***

Camp awoke alone in their bed. Jenny's side was cold. Wherever she was, she'd been gone for a while. He got up and went in search of her, but when it was clear she was nowhere on the property, he called her cellphone. She didn't answer. He called the hospital, but she wasn't there. He drove to her home in Baton Rouge, but that proved a bad choice; she hadn't been there either. The thought crossed his mind that she was the type to dive into work to escape, so he called both the lounge and the worksite, to no avail. She'd vanished.

He'd called Clay to see if he could get any information by running background information through the aid of one of his police friends. He didn't know what else to do.

He was relieved when Clay texted him her childhood home address; she was listed as the current owner on the tax rolls. The property was twenty miles outside of town in secluded pine woods. When Camp turned onto the road, he saw her car and was instantly relieved. He wondered where she could go—the house couldn't be safely explored. He got out of the car. The wind carried the smell of old wood char to his nostrils.

Camp heard a rhythmic squeaking and followed the sound around to the back of the house. There, under a pecan tree, Jenny swung on a tire, her legs pushing just hard enough to keep her moving. He crossed the yard and stood in front of her. When she looked up, he saw her tear-stained face.

She sat quietly swinging and although he had many questions, he didn't prod her. He dropped to the ground and leaned against a thick pine, content simply to offer his support. After twenty minutes or so, she started to talk.

"We used to make smiley-face pancakes on our birthdays. Didn't matter whose birthday either—Mom, Dad, me, Andrew. We all got pancakes. It was hard when they died. Andrew didn't understand death, not in the typical sense. I didn't understand it much myself at eighteen."

She sighed, but kept speaking. "He didn't understand when I told him our parents weren't coming back. He just kept asking over and over where had they gone and when would they be home. I tried to associate death with tangible things, but I wasn't very good at it.

"He'd lost his Snoopy thermos on the first day of kindergarten. The lost thermos was an issue because he was obsessed with Snoopy. When I told him our parents weren't coming back, just like his Snoopy thermos never did, he went ballistic. He was worried about the pancakes. He said they wouldn't be here for pancakes on their birthdays. Even though he was just a kid, when he got like that, he could do some damage. He attacked me. Then we went at each other. He pulled my hair and scratched my face. I beat on him any way I could get a punch in. That was how the first few years went."

Jenny gazed out across the field and seemed to go even farther away. Camp waited patiently for her to come back.

"I didn't want him. I know it's selfish, but everything had been taken from me in an instant. My future was now his, only his, and so I resented him. I was too young. I didn't seek help or even accept any help that was offered. The school sent a woman out, and she showed me how to set up schedules and routines." She laughed, the sound dry and humorless. "I had never been a keeper of any of those things, and I thought no one could force me to do more, so I didn't employ the strategies. After all, I'd made the ultimate sacrifice. I had no more to give."

Camp pushed back against the tree trunk, willing himself not to go to her. He didn't know what to do, so he didn't do anything. She blamed herself for so many things, so many events and feelings beyond her power to deal with them, but he knew if he tried to reach out to her, she would shut down.

"A number of times—shit, all the time—I had these thoughts that it would have been easier if he'd died in the fire too." Her tears started to fall again. "And of course it *would* have been easier on me, but who wishes that on her brother? Who wishes for something even worse on someone who has no control over the way his brain processes life? Who thinks such evil thoughts about a helpless little boy who'd lost his parents and who had no one but a spoiled sister to watch out for him?" She dragged a hand across her face, wiping away the tears. And then she fell silent again.

Camp closed his eyes, wanting to mend her broken heart. Wanting to keep his own from shattering. But it was too late. His heart had been bound to hers when she'd first called him Mr. St. Martin in that polite Southern voice she'd used to put him in his place. He would forever feel her pain and her joy as if they were his own. Feel her despair. Hear her heart beat in sorrow or in happiness.

They were linked, truly family, in a way that went beyond a mere legal joining. They belonged to one another. And he would do anything to see her heart healed.

"When I realized he was the only remaining link I had to my parents and, like it or not, he was my only family, it all started to change. *I* started to change. I went with him to therapy. I employed the strategies they gave me. We became active members of the autism society. It all helped. I had people to talk to and our life got better. I attended college while he was at school, and we fell into a routine."

She looked at Camp. "Things didn't stay on top, though. I met someone at school. I thought I was being given another chance at a happy life. He was nurturing and sincere. He loved Andrew and me. I couldn't believe it. We were going to be a family. One night he was on his way home from Orange Beach in Alabama. We'd wanted to see each other as soon as possible, so he drove late into the night. He was tired or careless. Maybe he even fell asleep. Whatever the cause, he careened off a bridge and drowned. I had to tell Andrew. He had a meltdown."

She turned away again and pumped her legs until she was swinging fast enough to set the rope whining against the tree.

"My grieving has always been overshadowed by Andrew's, always had to take second place, but I wasn't prepared to let him take this away from me. We fought verbally. Physically. Emotionally." Jenny gasped for breath before saying, "I told him I wished he'd slip into a coma, then I'd finally be happy. He left that night. Ran away. They found him at the defunct railroad crossing. He was prepared to jump to the ground. He kept saying he needed to be in a coma." Her breath caught. "Camp, I willed him into a coma."

Noting the look in her eyes, Camp knew there was nothing he could say that she would listen to. Not tonight. But he was done listening to her beat herself up for being a human in situations that would break the average man or woman. He was done letting her heap blame on herself. He scooped her up, put her in his truck, and started the drive home. She fell asleep next to him. Exhausted.

When they returned to the estate, Camp called Clay to check Andrew's status. No change.

Camp told his brother he'd found Jenny and related that she needed to be taken care of. Clay would stay at the hospital as long as Camp needed him there.

Camp started a bath. He stripped Jenny from her clothes and lowered her into the water. He heard her soft voice ask, "Camp, why do you want to be with me?"

"God, Jenny, there are so many reasons. Let me see if I can get you to understand it as I do."

He rested his chin on his hands at the side of the tub, praying for the right words, knowing that words straight from the heart were all he had to offer.

"I want to be enveloped in passion, but passion isn't easy. It's manic, it's obsessive, it's angry, it's compulsive. Passion can even make a man suffer and agonize. But in passion is life. If our lives were easy, they wouldn't be full of passion. Before you, my life was easier, but I hated every day. My life was apathy and indifference."

Camp leaned over Jenny in the tub and turned off the water. "You have great passion. You have fight. Hell, when I met you, we were fighting. You stood your ground next to me and fought for what you thought was right. You challenged me. You were responsive to me. When I met Andrew, I saw all of those qualities in him too. I couldn't wait for us to start our lives together, the three of us. I believe Andrew will fight to get back to us. And when he does, we will be there together, you and me, to welcome him back."

She cried a little at his admission or maybe at her brother's situation—he didn't know which. But over the last several weeks he'd learned her nuances and rhythms, and he knew she was done asking questions and laying the blame at her own feet. She soaked in the heat of the tub, and he helped her wash. When it was time to dress, she was still upset, so he quietly offered his help there too. When they arrived at the hospital, all of Camp's family was still there supporting and waiting.

Cash and Isa came up to them and distributed hugs all around. Isa shared a knowing look with Cash and then pulled Jenny over to a quiet spot in the corner. He offered up a little prayer for Isa and thanked God she was at the hospital. It was clear after only a few minutes that she'd eased Jenny's lingering anxiety. Jenny was smiling at something Isa said when other members of his family migrated toward the women.

He knew Jenny was overwhelmed by the love they had for Camp and by proxy, for her and Andrew. But it was a gentle, supportive love. And he recognized when she noted that very thing. She relaxed and allowed the rest of his family to see to her needs, bringing her coffee and food and even pillows.

At around four in the morning, there was an update. Andrew was coming around. The doctors said he would be moved to a regular room and they would be permitted to see him, but no more than two family members at a time.

As they walked down the hall to Andrew's room, Jenny looked nervously around. The nurse told them he was in room 112 and Jenny stopped walking to ask Camp why he thought Andrew had tried to jump Dreamer. He didn't know why, but told her they would ask him.

"Do you think . . . Was it to hurt himself like that time at the railroad tracks?"

"No, baby. I don't think he'd do that with Dreamer. Not to hurt himself. Not to hurt her."

They walked into Andrew's room, and Camp gave Andrew the Tennessee walker resin figurine that he'd loved as a boy.

"There you go, buddy. Now you've got a horse in here with you."

Andrew said, "Tennessee walker."

"That's right."

"Camp?"

"Yeah, Andrew?"

"Is Dreamer dead? Is she not coming back like Mom and Dad?"

Jenny flinched at his question.

Camp looked down at Andrew, as pale as the sheets he lay against, and smiled. "Andrew, Dreamer is fine. She's worried about you, is all. Why were you trying to jump her? You know that's against the rules."

"Jumping is against the rules." Andrew looked down at the figurine in his hand. "Mr. Camp?"

"Yes, Andrew?" Camp sat on the bed facing Andrew.

"I was going out for the pancake stuff. I was going to come back."

"Pancakes?"

"It was pancake day. I wanted to make Jenny happy because she's always mad."

Jenny's body shuddered and tears fell from her eyes. She walked up to her brother in the bed and kissed his cheek. Then she turned to Camp.

"Today is the anniversary of our parents' deaths. We'd started having their pancakes on the anniversary of that day." She hummed softly, stroking Andrew's arm until his eyes closed and his head tilted to the side.

Still looking at Andrew, still stroking his arm, she spoke to Camp.

"Andrew was good with numbers. When that date came around, he would get upset. It was the only thing I could think to do to keep him from having a meltdown. Since we started the tradition, he's dealt better with that day."

Camp caressed her arm, much as she stroked Andrew's.

Jenny might not know it, but she'd given Andrew a priceless gift, one that no doubt cost her plenty in terms of peace of mind. She would never be allowed to put that day behind her. But her gift had given Andrew something other than death to focus on.

His woman was generous beyond measure.

CHAPTER 9

After a week in the hospital, Andrew was released. They brought him home to the estate, and Camp took him to visit Dreamer in the paddock. Dreamer greeted Andrew with a nicker, and then she blew air in his face.

Jenny watched the exchange between Camp and Andrew from the porch. Mr. St. Martin, Cliff, joined her.

"Andrew's a good boy," he said.

Jenny smiled at Cliff. "Camp is good with him."

"He is. You know there are people in this world who need to have a purpose, a reason to exist."

Jenny didn't understand where he was going with his comment, so she just kept quiet. It had been a while since she'd gotten fatherly advice, but she recognized the approach.

"Camp is one of those people, always has been. That's why I was able to groom him for the family business. He organizes his mind and focuses it to achieve an intended outcome. In one case, it was to one day run our contracting company. I can see that same determination and focus now, with you and Andrew. He's always been a quiet brooder, and he's obsessive about what's his. He can get controlling and be consuming. He needs a woman who would appreciate those qualities and not stifle them. When he flourishes, he does great things. I only say this, Jenny, because if you are looking for a future, that future is here. Not only would you gain Camp, but you would also have the St. Martin clan to help you. You wouldn't have to be alone any longer." Cliff looked into her soul and asked, "Will you think about it?"

"Cliff, I love your son. And I agree with every word you just said. But he deserves someone fresh, someone with a clean history. Someone without baggage. It's because I love him that I should set him free."

"Bullshit." He snapped his fingers. "He needs someone with passion, someone who makes him feel alive. He needs someone who can accommodate a love like his. It's deep, strong, and too intense for most. But not for you. I've seen you with him. You need him just as much as he needs you. You and Andrew came to him with nothing, with no one. Now you have all of this." He waved his hands across the landscape. "I sense you pulling away. Don't do it, Jenny. You are part of this now. Part of him. And he is part of you. If you leave, you leave one half of each of you behind."

Well shit. How'd he know she was planning on bolting? Would have already, but with Andrew things took extra time. She thought over Cliff's words. It was all very practical and it made sense. Her body, her mind, her heart all wanted to believe in this life they offered her, but there was a quiet small part of her that wouldn't.

***

Camp jogged up to the porch, joining Jenny and his dad. He bent to kiss Jenny on the cheek.

"Hey, baby."

He studied them. They seemed intent. "What's up?"

"I was just telling Jenny that Andrew seems to have made a full recovery."

"Yeah, he has." But no damned way was that what had the two of them so solemn.

Campbell Lee St. Martin was no fool. He knew Jenny was restless. She was overwhelmed by what she hadn't known for years: friends, family, love, hope. And overwhelmed people searched for a way out.

But Camp had a plan for her. Clay, Cash and his father had been instrumental in helping him get the plan quite literally off the ground.

When his father recognized the connection Jenny and Camp had, he'd told Camp he was happy for him and confided that he'd been wrong to encourage him to marry Kim. Camp knew that everything his dad did for the family, he did out of unquestioning love and devotion. He'd only wanted to see Camp happy.

Now his dad smiled and said, "I'll bring the truck around so you can get loaded."

"Get loaded?" Jenny inquired.

"We're taking a trip."

***

"Camp, when can I take the bandana off?"

Camp had needed to blindfold Jenny in order to carry out his plan. She hadn't minded at first, but he sensed her growing frustration.

"When I say you can."

"But we're in a plane."

They *were* in a plane. His father had secured a private flight for the two of them. Camp was taking her to Las Vegas where he was going to marry her and where, if need be, he would buy a tracking device to hook to her in place of a ring. Whatever it took to keep her from running.

When they landed, a limo waited to take them to the apartment Cash kept in town. Cash, with his connections, had helped set up everything, down to the dress.

In the apartment the blinds had been drawn, and Camp removed the bandana from Jenny's eyes. She immediately started looking around. He walked to the refrigerator and found the champagne his brother had ordered. He uncorked a bottle and poured them each a glass. Camp hadn't really thought through the next stage of his plan because it depended on what inducements Jenny needed to go along with the plan. He hoped she'd agree wholeheartedly with everything, but he wasn't counting on it. He did think that plying her, and himself, with a little liquid courage couldn't hurt.

He handed a champagne flute to Jenny and toasted, "To us." She drank that down and Camp refilled her glass.

She eyed him suspiciously. He sat on the sofa while she wandered around the living room, fingering various knickknacks. When she crossed in front of the couch, she asked, "So, Camp, what are we doing here?" She ran her index finger across his collarbone through the thin T-shirt he wore. Then she backed out of his reach.

"Come back here and I'll show you."

Eyebrows raised, she stepped between his legs.

"Take off your shorts."

Jenny swallowed the contents of her second glass of champagne and did as he commanded.

"Panties too."

Once she was bared from the waist down, Camp patted his lap and she crawled up and he cradled her in his arms. He closed his eyes, inhaling her scent. The familiarity soothed him, but he wondered if he shouldn't have poured himself a second glass of champagne. His future was wrapped up in this woman. What if she didn't want what he wanted? What he needed?

Camp set his fingers on her sex and worked his fingers in. She was hot and already wet. He stroked her clit with his thumb while massaging her slit with his fingers. When he'd worked her into a lather and had her panting for breath, he slid out from beneath her and laid her out on the couch. Her eyes were hooded, her body fluid.

"I've brought some toys."

Her eyes grew wide and snapped to life.

Camp reached behind the couch to retrieve the bag he'd carried in with them. Clay had selected the toys.

Jenny sat up.

"Lie down or I'll tie you up, spank you, gag you, or blindfold you. Whatever it takes."

Jenny inhaled a ragged breath and lay back against the cushions.

"Good girl."

Camp tapped her clit with his fingertips. Jenny gasped.

"Pull your legs to your chest."

She pulled her knees in close to her body.

"Spread your knees."

Jenny spread her knees so that she was completely exposed to Camp. God, every time she did that and he saw all of her, he thought *that belongs to me.* He was obsessed with her.

"Stay like that—don't move—or I'll bind you, I swear it. Do you understand?"

Jenny whispered, "Y-yes."

Camp wondered if he was pushing too hard but when she licked her lips, when he watched her eyes follow his every move, he bit back a satisfied grin.

Camp poured oil into his hands before applying it to Jenny's body. He massaged her hips and her thighs and when she started to writhe, he massaged the oil into her pussy. Then he pulled the cold, egg-shaped metal vibrator from the bag. He rubbed it between his hands to make it slick with oil. When it touched Jenny's sex, she gasped. Camp worked the tip in first. When the egg was almost halfway inside, Jenny contracted and her walls swallowed up the egg.

"Fuck," Camp cried. He was instantly hard.

Now he had to insert the bullet vibrator into her ass. The bullet was wider than any one of his fingers, which he knew to be the only thing ever to penetrate her ass. And with the egg in her pussy, there wasn't as much room to work with as usual. Still, he wanted to use both toys. Clay had said any woman would consent to anything if she was on the brink and her partner used the remotes to activate the vibrators at an opportune moment.

Camp oiled his fingers and rubbed a good amount of oil into Jenny's bottom. When he slid his middle finger slowly into her bud, she moaned. He could feel the hardness from the egg in her cunt. She was already contracting. When she did, her ass dilated, and he added his index finger, widening her sufficiently. Jenny growled his name low in her throat. Shit. Camp was leaking precum and he vaguely wondered about his ability to get through the ordeal without creaming in his pants. Clay hadn't said anything about *him* being unable to hold back when he was teasing Jenny this way. He forced his mind to think about an upcoming project and the problems he'd already anticipated for it until he had his body under control.

Then he turned back to Jenny.

Her body was thrumming with energy as Camp pumped his fingers in her ass. He thought she might be close, but it wouldn't do to bring her to release just yet. He removed his fingers and brought the bullet vibrator to her oil-slicked bud. He pushed the tip through the muscle, and she contracted. He pushed the vibrator until it was fully seated inside her.

"Jenny?" He looked into her eyes. They were glazed over. "Baby?"

In a hoarse whisper she said, "Camp, I'm so full. Please . . . I need you."

"I know, baby, we're almost there."

Moaning, she dropped her head back on the couch. Camp pulled her legs down and she shuddered and quivered. Camp soothed her, running his hands over her, then he gently kissed her lips and her closed eyes.

"Sit up."

Camp helped her upright and dressed her in the cream fitted cocktail dress that Cash had ordered from one of the hotel's boutiques. Jenny didn't make a sound or ask a question. She just watched him with hooded eyes.

He led her to the bathroom and she brushed her hair and teeth while he dressed quickly in black dress trousers and a blue silk shirt.

When he was ready, he patted his pocket to ensure he had the rings and the vibrator remotes. He ran a shaking hand down Jenny's arm, traced her lips.

"We've gotta walk now, baby." He helped her to the elevator. The high-rise Cash lived in was connected to a large casino. They went down to the lobby level and passed through the veranda shops.

When they arrived at the wedding chapel, Camp took her hands in his. "Jenny, you look beautiful."

He wanted to get down on one knee, but he was afraid that would give her too much wiggle room and he didn't want her to bolt, because he feared she'd never come back. Even he had to admit he was a little intense. Still, his girl was unflappable. She was constantly fighting him and anyone else who got in the way of what she needed to accomplish. She would make a great St. Martin.

"Jennifer Roberts, we're going to walk through these doors and our lives are going to forever be changed. You're going to marry me. Now. Here. You will say yes and I do. Those are the only options. Tell me you understand."

The color in her cheeks was dark, and her eyes were liquid fire. They narrowed to slits as she smoldered at him. But Camp was no longer afraid. Her eyes didn't burn with anger, they raged with love. A fierce, active, ever-flaming love. He grinned back at her. His baby girl was going to fight him all the way to the altar, but it was a battle they were both going to win.

Camp pulled the door open and escorted Jenny through. The room was set up like a small traditional chapel, with six pews on each side and an aisle down the center. Elvis waited for them at the end of the aisle. Camp and

Jenny walked to the front, hand in hand, consensually. He caught a grin on her face when they stopped in front of the make-do alter.

When the time came for Jenny to answer the question *Do you take this man*, Camp had his hand in his pocket, one finger on the remote. She shook her head and opened her mouth, and Camp turned on the egg-shaped vibrator inside her pussy. She made an incoherent sound, and Elvis asked the question a second time. When she opened her mouth again, Camp turned on the vibrating bullet in her ass. His poor baby girl. If she would just comply, he wouldn't have to do this to her. He could see the energy charging through her body. She closed her eyes and swallowed back a growl. Elvis asked if she was feeling ill. She denied sickness. He asked again if she'd take Camp, and this time she said yes. Smart girl. Camp turned off the egg vibrator, but left the bullet on at its lowest setting.

The rings were exchanged and they were proclaimed husband and wife. When Camp bent down to kiss his bride, she bit down on his lip hard enough to draw blood. He grinned, wanting instead to laugh.

Signatures were required on the marriage certificate and when Jenny only tapped her pen against the paper, Camp turned up the setting on the vibrator in her ass. She signed the paper and slammed the pen to the desk. And then she winked at Elvis. Evidentially she'd been playing him. He'd get her back for that later on in the apartment.

Camp smiled at the Elvis impersonator and accepted from him the most precious piece of paper he would ever hold in his hands.

Camp escorted Jenny, his wife, to the elevator bank. They boarded the elevator in an electrically charged silence. When the doors closed, Camp said, "Good evening, Mrs. St. Martin." Jenny jumped into Camp's arms and wrapped her legs around his waist. She started rubbing her sex frantically against him. "Mmm, now this is what I call a consummation," Camp murmured.

When the elevator door opened, he stepped into the hall with his wife wrapped provocatively around him. Standing in front of Cash's apartment door, Camp was fishing for the keys when a couple passed them in the hallway.

"How do you do?" he said. "Just married. Wife can't keep her hands off of me for a second."

The couple snickered as they passed.

He stumbled into the apartment and clothes started coming off. He tugged at Jenny's dress and she ripped his shirt. When they stood naked before one another, her hands sensually roamed his torso and neck, eventually snaking into his hair. He moved in to kiss her and she pulled his hair hard and ran out of the room. He found her as she was jumping up onto the bed. He caught her by the foot and pulled her down beneath him. She squealed. And then she was giggling. He held one of the vibrator remotes in his hand. When he turned it on, she stopped giggling and started howling.

"I love you, Jenny. You're mine forever now."

"Camp, are you gonna bloody consummate this marriage or sweet talk me to death?"

"Sweet talked to death. It wouldn't be such a bad way to go, would it?"

Jenny pressed her left hand against his chest, stared at the ring on her finger. Camp adjusted his balance so he could wrap his left hand around hers. He felt the weight of their love pressing against his heart. He felt his heartbeat pressing back against Jenny's warm skin.

"Camp, I love you. I've never been this happy." She smiled into his eyes. "Thank you for marrying me." She released a long sigh. "Thank you for loving me." She placed her lips at his ear and whispered, "I would have married you without the aid of toys."

Camp felt the buildup of tears behind his lashes, but at the same time he couldn't hold back his smile.

"You know we're going to have to have a second wedding for the family."

"We are?"

"Oh yes. I was thinking on the estate. Plus I need to buy you a diamond."

Jenny's eyes sparkled. "I've never had a diamond before—it'll be my first."

"The start of many firsts, Mrs. St. Martin."

Camp kissed Jenny, and then they consummated their first marriage to one another.

***

Gina Watson